SHARED

A MFM MÉNAGE ROMANTIC EROTIC NOVELLA
(BEACHSIDE MÉNAGE BOOK 1)

MAISIE BEASLEY

Copyright © 2021 by Maisie Beasley

All rights reserved.

No part of this book may be reproduced in any form or by any electronic or mechanical means, including information storage and retrieval systems, without written permission from the author, except for the use of brief quotations in a book review.

CHAPTER 1

MILLIE

"He's watching you again."

The ocean air smells of sand, salt, and the suntan oil that glistens across my boyfriend's thick shoulders and broad, bronzed chest. In the same breath that I turn my head to face him, he rolls onto his side. A single bead of sweat slips down his neck and rolls downward, arcing over strong pecs and into the dark dusting of hair that sprinkles underneath his collarbone. The urge to lean over and suck that drop between my lips, and to lavish the heavy muscles of his chest with the keen attention of my tongue, swells so strongly that it takes serious effort to merely lick my lips in response.

We've been together three years, James and I, but my desire for him hasn't waned a bit. I'm starting to think it never will.

He reciprocates those thoughts exactly, evident in the soft, pleased sigh that escapes his mouth. His sunglasses obscure his eyes, merely mirroring my own reflection back at me, but I know his gaze lingers on my lips. I can simply feel it, and the knowledge wells a deep heat in my stomach that only grows as he shifts across the fine, white sand to clear the few inches that separate us. "You've noticed this time, haven't you?" he asks, his voice plunged lower still, and he passes a wide hand down the bare column of my spine with fingers light as air. He bends towards me, drops a kiss onto the top of one shoulder, and allows his head to linger near mine. "You can't deny it anymore, because there's no way you could have missed the way he stared at you when you came downstairs in this fucking bikini." His hand comes to rest at the line of my bottoms, placed more on my ass than my back—and my bare ass, at that. The slick, baby blue fabric barely covers anything. "He looked like he could hardly contain himself, and I don't blame him. You look *unreal*."

James has said similar things about other men, and often. His rampant jealousy—a jealousy mixed with a strong inclination of pride—had become something of a running joke among our friends from the moment we'd started dating our senior year of college. During nights out, in the middle of classes, seated in the dining hall—it hadn't mattered, and it still doesn't. He's remained convinced that other men want me in the same way that he does, with the same single-minded determination and deep conviction and obsession that has kept typically us more in bed than out of it.

And yet he's never sounded as pleased about it as he does when it comes to his best friend, Luke, who lays sprawled out across a beach chair several feet away. Just as I can feel James' eyes on me, his chin tipped to watch the progress of his hand across my skin, I swear I can feel Luke's too, even as he laughs loudly with our other friends.

My insides quickly set aflame, burning with a combination of desire and shame that I've felt for years when around James and Luke together. "We're in public," I remind James as his fingers slip lower, gliding along the almost-indecent cut of my bikini bottoms. Despite my words, his fingertips burn a pattern into my eager flesh. "And *you* picked out this suit, so don't—"

He cuts me off neatly. "You didn't seem to care that we were in public last night when you sucked my cock on the balcony," he says against my ear, and my stomach twists. Instantly, I'm hurtled back twelve hours in the past, lunging face-first into the memory of his panting encouragement and his hands messy in my hair and his thick cock deep in the back of my throat. Desire floods my mouth and bikini bottoms at the same time, summoned by the mere thought of his salty taste and his sheer desperation that had sent his voice into tatters from the moment I'd reached for the buckle of his belt. "And with everyone just below us on the deck," he adds, his tone mockingly judgmental. He slides one powerful leg across both of mine, and the fine, dark hairs that line his leg tickle my smooth calves. His hips press into my side, and I feel him growing there, stiffening as he surely recalls all the same thoughts. "How naughty of you, Millie. Tell me—" His index finger drags along the curve where my ass meets my thigh, and my back arches outside my control, desperate to press into his hand. He groans quietly, a hoarse sound trapped somewhere in the base of his throat, and he presses a kiss underneath my jaw. "Were you thinking about Luke down there with everyone else? Did you imagine him finding us, or him hearing me sing your praises as you fucking sucked my soul out of my cock? Did you—"

"James!" His name slips from between my teeth, a hiss that could be taken as pleasure or rebuke. He certainly takes it as the prior, evident in a second low, throaty sound pressed into my neck as he palms my ass. "You—"

He shifts again with a subtle thrust of his hips that seems instinctual. "I told him about it this morning," he says. The wicked words brand my skin, burning with the same intensity as his tongue when he locates a familiar spot on my neck and gives a brief, taunting swipe that makes the muscles of my pussy jump. "Before breakfast, I told him about how you sucked on my balls until I begged you to put me out my misery, and then how you finally took me so deep in your throat that your eyes watered. I told him how you told me to fuck your pretty little mouth, and how you spread your perfect legs for me and had three fingers in your pussy before I could even tell you to do it. I told him how you pleaded with me to blow my load in your mouth, how greedy you were to swallow every drop, but how there's nothing like coming deep inside you, so I bent you over the balcony railing and took you that way. I told him that he probably would have seen you if he'd looked up, and he could have watched your tits bounce and seen you put your hand over your mouth as you tried to keep yourself from screaming my name when you came. And I told him how when *I* came, I— Jesus, babe, you had me squeezed so fucking tight that I could have passed out right there. Just thinking about it *—fuck—*"

He has me breathless by then, with all thoughts of propriety swiftly set aside as I tangle my hand in the dark, messy hair that gathers at the nape of his neck. Without hesitation, his mouth finds mine, and a familiar dance ensues of tongues slowly stroking and lips softly sliding and teeth gently grazing before he tilts my body, drawing me off my stomach and more towards my side so he can slide a sun-soaked, finely-built leg between both of mine.

Ocean breeze blows past one peaked nipple, reminding me of something I'd forgotten the second he'd first put his hands on me: I had untied the back of my top.

"For fuck's sake—"

Only Luke's voice could pull me back to reality in that moment, although it doesn't exactly quell my desire.

Something soft hits my back as I hurriedly extract my

legs from James' and press my chest back to my towel. Luke has thrown something, presumably, and I turn my head to find that he's launched his shirt in protest. Like James, he wears a pair of dark sunglasses that hide the exact path of his gaze, but he has his eyes somewhere on my body—at James' hand on my ass? At the exposed side of my breast? At the bare length of my back?

It doesn't matter. Just his attention on me, paired with the tight hold of his jaw, is enough to send my legs squeezing together for some hint of relief.

James feels it. In turn, his thumb once again grazes along the line of my swimsuit that curves over one cheek.

"Perverts, the pair of you," Luke says—or declares, rather, as he leans forward in his chair. In contrast to James, whose mere shoulders could block many a doorway and whose dark hair and eyes match the night sky, Luke is longer, leaner, more wiry but still powerful. He's all gold, from tousled hair to tanned skin to eyes the color of hot honey. The veins in his arms bulge as he swings his feet onto the sand and then presses his elbows onto his knees. "I don't know why we brought you with us on this trip. You'd think after all these years that you'd lay off each other once in a while, but—"

I hear James' smile from behind me as he speaks. "Don't judge, bro. You wouldn't lay off her either."

Our other friends—Kyle, Aaron, Grant, and Bryan, and my best friends Cassie and Annette—all sit in various spots and poses behind Luke. Everyone else looks locked in some deep conversation, but Cassie's neck lifts from its lounging position. Subtly, she plucks one of her earbuds from her ear.

Luke doesn't miss a beat. "I don't know anyone who would," he says shortly, and he stands. "I need to cool off."

He rises to his feet and jogs towards the sparkling blue waters that lap onto the shore. He cuts a striking figure that turns more than one interested head as he passes several clusters of women our age, as well as some younger and far older still.

I can see why. Even if he didn't glint under the sun like some bronzed god carved of blocks of sinewy muscle, he'd still hang heavily underneath his swimming trunks. I have just enough time to see him adjust himself unselfconsciously, one hand gripping the thick line of his cock that presses up through the navy material, before he disappears from view.

James gives my ass another squeeze, and it draws my attention back to the chiseled lines of his face. In contrast, his consideration remains locked on Luke's retreating back. "I know you saw that," he says, the words once again nearly whispered. "He's been hard since you untied your top."

My breath comes in sharply. "I hadn't noticed."

But he had, and he sounds...what?

Intrigued?

Pleased?

Aroused?

He's certainly the latter, his cock still hard against my hip, and it twitches as he touches my face with his free hand, the one attached to the arm he leans on with a casualness I know he doesn't feel. He skates his thumb across my parted lips, and I know what he wants. I draw it into my mouth instinctually, roll my tongue across the callused tip, and taste the salt and sand that clings to his skin. He swears faintly, a low, muted, *"Fuck,"* that sends a fresh wave of arousal through my bloodstream. "You want him," he says, his thumb pressing further to sink into my mouth. "Admit it."

I freeze, my tongue twisted around his short nail and my breath swollen in my throat.

It's not the first time he's voiced something similar in the years that we've dated—some mention of Luke's eyes on me; or a teasing remark on the obvious chemistry that crackles between us; or even a declaration that *Luke* certainly wants *me*, even if I hardly believe it. He even brings it up sometimes when we fuck, in what sounds like a fantasy that has somehow grown further and further into a potential reality without me even realizing it. Yet he's never twisted things the other way around, claiming that *I* want *Luke,* and certainly never with such staunch belief leaking from his every pore. He sounds like he simply *knows* I want him, knows it as deeply as arousal swirls in my insides and stains my cheeks, and guilt swiftly follows. Wanting Luke usually ends up feeling that way.

He must see some note of that in my face, because his jaw softens suddenly, and his mouth curls upwards into a smile I can only qualify as tender. "It's okay," he says, and he brushes a kiss over the bridge of my nose, a familiar caress of his lips that often wakes me in the morning. "It's okay," he repeats, kissing higher to press his lips between my brows. His thumb slips from my mouth, and his hand rises to wind into the thick curls that have escaped across the back of my neck. "If it were anyone else, I'd hate it. I'd *hate* it. But—" He offers me a gentle caress that slides easily across the heat gathered at the base of my neck. "I don't mind with Luke. He's—you know, he's basically my brother. And—"

He's so close that I can smell the faint mint of his chapstick, chapstick he's stolen directly from my lips. "Say it," I breathe when he falters, and his teeth gleam brilliantly in the grin that steals across his face.

"How wet are you right now?"

Embarrassment and guilt have both fled, chased away by pure need. "Drenched," I tell him, and his grin flickers as he swallows. I know the look that must cloud his eyes, but I tug his sunglasses from his face to check for certain. Sure enough, lust clouds eyes dark as coal, and his gaze flickers back and forth between each of my eyes, searching, hunting, hungry. "I'm *dripping*. Take me home and find out."

His tongue darts out across his lips to drag slowly. "Later," he promises darkly. "Later. Right now, I need to go make fun of Luke." He reaches down in between us, his own adjustment much more discreet than Luke's as he presses his erection flat against his stomach and tucks it into the waistband of his trunks. "But, just for the record—"

He kisses me again, another slow, careful meeting of mouths that makes a promise with his tongue that I can nearly hear, although he says no words. His body feels like one solid slab of marble pressed into mine, with his muscles pulled so tight that it will almost certainly take hours of effort to unspool the tension that ropes across his shoulders and down his arms and through his hips and into his legs. I want nothing more than to take those hours, to use my hands and tongue and pussy to drag every last bit of rigidity from his body and every last sound from his lips.

Somehow, he knows—perhaps because he always knows, because he knows *me,* knows me in the depths of my soul and down to my shaking core like no other man ever has. "Later," he says a third time, an assurance against my lips, and he says it more promisingly still. "But, for the record…I wouldn't mind it. With Luke."

He has me so distracted by his hand drifting to my hip that the words hardly register. When they finally do, they crash through the hazy longing in my brain like a hammer smashing through a wall. "Mind what?"

He shrugs a single shoulder, and his other hand slides up to bury fully in my hair. "You know." He licks his lips again. "You and him. You know I've thought about it before. It's hard not to when he's constantly staring at your tits or your ass. He has been for years, since before we even started dating, and…I've wondered what it would be like to share your body with someone who would appreciate you. Worship you. Like I do."

As if his words don't give enough away—or the way he says them, all thick desire that reads in the depths of his eyes and the hold of his jaw—his cock does. Tucked securely into his waistband or not, it throbs against my hip, and it takes everything in me not to reach out and touch him.

God, I love him. I love him so much that it *hurts*.

"James—" I say a second time, my throat tight and my voice constrained, and it doesn't matter that dozens of other people surge around us on the beach, filling the air with shouts and laughter and shrieks as waves crash repeatedly under it all. Suddenly, we're the only two people there, and we're teetering on the edge of something intense and irrevocable and—

Something I want badly. *Very* badly.

"I want you," I tell him, the words rushed together, and his hand contracts on my hip. "God, I want you. Take me home. Take me home and give me your mouth for five minutes. I don't even know if it'll take me that long, because I'm—fuck, baby, I'm *aching* for you. Make me come and then you can have me however you want me. Use me. I want—"

Victory washes over him, flooding his handsome features and dripping down the tightly-coiled springs of his body. "Later," he says again, a fourth time, and I've suddenly never hated a word more. He sits up and then leans over me, his strong arms on either side of my body as his chest presses into my back and rubs tantalizingly, skin brushing and creating sparks just like when he takes me slowly from behind. He drops a kiss to my temple and pauses for a moment with his nose buried in my hair. "I'm going to lick you clean later," he says throatily, and I whimper as my fingers grip his wrist. "And he's going to watch."

CHAPTER 2

JAMES

I'm hard for the rest of the day.

Even without looking at me, Luke clocks it by the time I join him in the water. He shakes wet hair from his face as I dive into a wave beside him. "Just go fuck her," he says before I can speak. A quiet note of frustration seeps into his tone. "One of us might as well enjoy this trip."

Stifling laughter comes difficultly. "Are you not having a good time?"

Another wave swells, and our bodies float with it. His mouth is a flat line, as flat as his response. "Not like you are."

He knows, of course. He knows every way I've ever fucked Millie, dating back to the first time I'd gotten her panties down and laid eyes on her perfect pussy. He knows that she's taken me deeper in her throat than any other woman ever has, and he knows that I'd happily forgo food in order to feast between her thighs. He knows that she'll sometimes tie me up and tease me for hours before finally making me come so hard that it liquifies my spine, and that, in turn, she lets me blindfold her and treat her as my plaything to use however I want. He knows countless stories, those he's listened to with rapt attention as many times as I've ever wanted to tell them to him—which is every story, if I'm honest. He knows she's the best fuck of my life—and the love of my life to boot—because I've told him so repeatedly. I've told him both because it's true, and—

Well, and because I love watching him squirm with barely-suppressed jealousy and desire; love watching the way his eyes sharpen when she comes into a room; love watching him flirt with her so blatantly that our friends have all questioned it to me more than once, their concerns spoken tentatively so as not to upset me at the implication that my two favorite people might betray me with each other.

It *should* upset me, probably, to know that my best friend gets off to thoughts of the love of my life, but it doesn't.

Honestly, I like it. I like it far more than I should, enough that the cool water hasn't stopped the throbbing in my cock.

Fuck, maybe I should have taken Millie home. Or maybe I should have taken her into the ocean with me—hastily tied her top back in place, thrown her over my shoulder, and tossed her slick body into the waves. Surely the churning water would hide enough for her to free my cock and jerk me off, or to wrap her long, silky legs around my waist and grind down until I come into my trunks like a fourteen-year-old.

It probably wouldn't even take long, by the feel of it, but I've always had a hair trigger when it comes to her. The years we've spent together have really only made that worse, not better.

A grin tugs the corners of my mouth. "She begged me to take her home," I tell him, and his throat contracts as the surging waves overtake his noisy swallow. "She said she was aching for me and begged for five minutes of my mouth. 'Use me,' she said, and she told me I could have her however I wanted once I made her come. You should have heard her. She was—"

A wave smacks me in the face, but not one given by Mother Nature. This one comes courtesy of Luke's hands and arms, and it's a large splash forcefully given. "Fuck off," he says, but without ire. "Fuck off and go do it, you idiot. Do it and then tell me about it so I can live vicariously through you."

Oh. *Interesting*.

He's long since stopped hiding his inability to keep his eyes off Millie, but he's never said anything *that* honest before.

He catches himself quickly. "It's the closest I'm going to get to getting laid," he adds, correcting himself, and he looks away from me as he treads water. "It's been—fuck, it's been *months*."

"Cassie and Annette are available."

He lets out a brief, rueful chuckle. "Millie would kill me."

"Probably, but not on their accounts. She'd kill you out of jealousy, more like."

He turns back to me at that, the movement of his head sharp, but I dive under the water before he can do much more than open his mouth. Let him chew on *that*.

I know what I'm doing. I know what I'm trying to orchestrate, a goal that has probably lurked in the subconscious part of my brain for far longer than I've admitted it to myself. And once I'd realized what I wanted and had finally come to terms with it myself—

"You're relentless," Millie had said to me early on, as our friendship struck up in a college literature course had quickly morphed into fantasies of her full lips wrapped around my cock and her perfect tits fitted into my hands and not the tight fabric of her t-shirts. She'd laughed as she'd said it, clearly more amused than put off by my determination to

get her out of the classroom and onto a date. That date had turned into a second, and then a third, and then a fourth—

By then, I'd introduced her to my friends, and I'd already noticed how Luke had watched her with the same open admiration I had. Still, he'd stopped commenting on her blatant desirability by the time she'd agreed to see me exclusively, which had happened quite quickly. Once I'd had a taste of her, I hadn't wanted to share.

Except—

As I'd told her, maybe with him, because I trust him. I trust him and love him like a brother, and, beyond that—

I'll do anything to make that woman come. I want what she wants, as simple as that, and I know she feels the same way, to the point that I'm not sure which one of us first thought up including Luke in some way or another. It's a real chicken-or-the-egg scenario, and I'm not sure which had come first—her desire for him, or my desire to see her with him—but I'm definitely the one about to make things happen.

For the rest of the day and into the night, they prowl around each other, and I watch.

Sun has colored Millie's cheeks, giving her the appearance of a constant flush that reminds me far too much of the way she looks when spread out underneath me and blissed out from my fingers or mouth or cock. She looks like sex personified, like a physical representation of all the filthy things I've done to her and all the filthier things yet to come, and I know I'm not the only one to notice. Surely none of the guys are immune to the bright sound of her laughter or the soft sway of her hair or—*Jesus*—the way she spreads lotion up one long leg and then the other in full view in the living room, cream smoothed up her ankle, and then her calf, and then her knee, and finally to where her dress hits at mid-thigh. Yet they hide it better, far better than they conceal admiring glances towards Cassie or Annette, and I know it's out of respect to me. The careful way Aaron averts his eyes when one slender strap slips down Millie's arm, revealing the top of one smooth, pert breast, says that much.

But Luke? Luke not only stares at every move she makes, his eyes like hot daggers, but he touches. He winds a thick curl around his finger, tugging it teasingly; he slides an arm over her shoulders, the embrace outwardly platonic; he takes over the job of rubbing the back of her neck when she shifts her hair aside to do it herself. Finally, well past midnight, he stands beside her at the kitchen island with their hips and sides and bared arms touching, and he laughs with her as she toys with a dish of ice cream. He stares mostly at her tongue passing over her spoon, although his eyes flick up to meet hers every time she says something he finds particularly amusing. More than once, she gives him *that look* as she licks chocolate slowly off the back of her spoon, that same challenging, promising, erotic look she gives me when she runs her tongue along the ridges of my cock, and—

She must know what she's doing. She must know *exactly* what she's doing—to both of us.

"I fold," Cassie says from my side, tossing her cards onto the table. I shift under the table, adjust my aching cock, and do the same. "I'm shit at this, and I'm ready for bed anyway."

They all head that way—Cassie, Annette, Grant, Bryan, Kyle and Aaron for the stairs, and Luke for the master suite just off the kitchen. He's offered it to me and Millie before, but it's his parents' place, so she'll never hear of taking it.

He looks reluctant as he twists the knob, and his eyes train on where Millie lingers by the counter, still scraping the last bits from her bowl with that damn spoon. "Keep it down, will you, kids?" he asks, his grin sardonic. "And wipe down wherever you end up fucking. That's all I ask."

Millie laughs, her head tipped back so that her hair

swings between her shoulder blades. "Whatever you say," she says, her cheeks flushing darker, and she glances towards me with a question in her eyes.

Where? she seems to ask, because she knows me well enough—knows *us* well enough, us together—to know that that's the only real consideration in place.

God, I love her.

"Come here," I tell her, scooting back a little from the table, and I beckon her with two fingers gently curved, the same way I often make her come.

Luke snorts quietly, and he disappears into his room without another word.

Well, whatever. If he's not quite ready to admit what he wants, I can help pull it out of him.

"Come here and ride me," I tell her, and I wait both for her response and also to hear Luke's steps fade across his bedroom on the other side of the closed door.

The prior comes, but the latter doesn't. "That's not what you promised me earlier," Millie says softly.

I can almost *see* Luke standing on the other side of the door with his ear pressed to the crack to listen intently. My cock twitches.

"Is that why you've been licking your spoon for the past hour? It wasn't terribly subtle."

A dimple flares in each cheek as she ducks her head. Her laughter comes out softly. "James—"

My name on her lips sparks something primal in me, just as it always has. "Was I the only one you were teasing?" I ask, rubbing a rough hand over my cock. Her eyes follow the motion and remain locked there as I stroke with short caresses through my shorts. "Babe." She jumps a little, as if pulled from a daze. "Who are you wet for?"

She whimpers, a pretty noise that goes directly to my cock. "You."

"Just me?"

"I—" She glances towards Luke's bedroom door with warning in her eyes. "It's not—"

"It gets you off, doesn't it? Knowing he wants you? Knowing he'd have you bent over the counter right now if he could? Knowing he's probably jerking off right now just at the memory of you practically deepthroating your spoon?"

She swallows, and that alone could undo me. Just that, not to mention what I feel when she nods.

"Say it, Mills."

"Yes," she whispers, the word spoken softly on exhale. "God, yes, but I—I feel *terrible* over it—"

I groan and grip my cock tighter as pleasure stacks on pleasure. "Don't feel terrible. It's hot. It's so hot. Just—get over here, get on the table, and spread your legs for me while you tell me about it."

I've never seen her move so fast in all my life.

"Fuck—" she says, a swear pressed against my lips as she wraps her sunkissed arms around my neck. "Fuck, James, *fuck*—"

She ends up in my lap instead of on the table, her pussy held tight against my cock, and I can feel her wetness even through my shorts and whatever flimsy scrap of underwear she'd put on after her shower. Desperate to feel her against me, I pull her dress up and mold my hands to her ass and tug, and she rewards me with another curse into my mouth as her hands scramble to pull my shirt up and off. Afterwards, her fingers spread across my shoulders, and then my arms, and then my chest, stroking and caressing and squeezing, each sound of pleasure a heady shot to my ego.

"I've been waiting for you *all day*," she says as her lips travel along my jaw and towards my ear. Her teeth catch my earlobe. "I should have just gotten myself off in the shower earlier, but I didn't, and—god, you're so *cruel* to make me wait this long—"

I can't suppress my smile. "I couldn't wait. That was the first thing I did when we got back from the beach."

She gasps, although if in outrage—real or mock—or from the increased pressure of my hands on her ass, I can't tell. "You should have let me watch," she says as her teeth nip slowly down my neck. "I love watching you touch yourself. It's the look on your face when you do it. It's seriously so hot—"

Again, I don't know where the idea begins and where it ends, which one of us has planted the seed and who has watered it, but the image of Luke eating her out while she watches me jerk off suddenly conjures to mind. I can almost *see* it—the pleasure on her face from his tongue, the pleasure in her eyes from how badly I want her, the pleasure tearing at her throat when she comes.

"Tell me what you thought about," she says, and her hips stutter when I slide my fingers underneath the thin waistband of her thong. "God—*baby*—"

That's my kryptonite, that endearment, and she knows it. I lift her off me, hoist her easily onto the table, and drag her to the edge. She rocks back on her elbows from the force, but she never falters. Her fingers eagerly lift the hem of her dress for me, and my mouth literally waters as I bend to lick the lotion from her thighs. She smells like sun and citrus and sex, and she leans back fully, her back pressed to the table one moment and then arching beautifully the next, as I drag my tongue across the delicate fabric separating me from her pussy.

Behind her, the door to Luke's bedroom cracks open.

I can't tell if she notices. Her pussy flexes under my tongue, begging for me to probe deeper, but it might have nothing to do with him. It might have everything to do with her hands winding into my hair, and nothing to do with the separation of his door from its frame. It's impossible to tell.

Still, I add for his benefit, "You're *dripping,* Mills." She moans in response. "You were soaking your panties for him, weren't you?"

"Yes," she says, and she lifts her hips, encouraging me to drag those same panties down her thighs. I don't. "Baby, *please—*"

I twist my tongue atop her clit. "What? Tell me what you want."

"I want you to take my panties down and fuck me—" She sounds almost angry, as frustrated as I've ever heard her, and it's the hottest fucking thing I can imagine. "With your fingers, with your tongue, with your cock—I don't care which. Just—oh, thank you, *thank you—*" She strokes my hair as gratitude falls from her throat, and her hips lift with even more intent as I hook my finger over the center of her panties and tug them down.

I shove them into the pocket of my shorts and stare at the slick lips of her pussy and further still, past her stomach and towards her covered, heaving breasts and the pink of her cheeks. "Do you want to know what I thought about when I was beating off in the shower today?" I ask her, and she nods keenly, her pussy still thrust upward. I reward her enthusiasm with a slow lick, but I stop just below her clit. She sighs, frustrated, and her fingers tug pleasurably in my hair. I offer her a second lick, and then a third, and then a forth, finally twisting my tongue around where she's attempted to bring me all along, and her legs clamp down around my head. "I thought about the way you'd whimper with my cock in your throat if Luke were fucking you from behind exactly like you like it—with your ass in the air and your hair in his fist and his cock absolutely *pounding* you—"

She gasps and sits up sharply, and, for a moment, I think

I've pushed her too far. But then she grabs me, hauls me to my feet, and pulls my shorts down so that my cock comes free. "Fuck me," she says, more a demand than a request, and her hand wraps around my swollen head, where precum offers more than enough slickness for her to slide her fist easily. She pumps a few times, each caress joined by moans of her own that I echo despite myself. "I need your cock. Fuck, baby, I *need* it. Hearing you talk like that, it's—God, it's almost *too* much—"

Pulling her hand away, I drag my cock between her thighs to slip just between her folds but never inside. I'm not sure who it torments more. No matter my restraint, I'm right there with her, swearing repeatedly under my breath as I slide the straps of her dress down to watch her breasts sway unencumbered. "Do you want that? Me and him? Together?"

I can see movement over her shoulder behind Luke's door, some shuffling shapes not easily identifiable in the dark room, but I don't need to truly see to know what goes on. It would take a man of steel not to crack and reach for his cock just under the spell of Millie's pleased whimpers, let alone the wet sounds between her thighs and the sight of her from behind with her back bare to him and her breasts free to me. I bend to run my tongue across one pebbled nipple, and she clutches the back of my head to hold me in place.

"Yes," she says, and, for a second, I think it's my groan I hear, but the tension of her fingers tells a different tale. I glance up to see her eyes pop open, and I know then.

It's Luke we hear, and the wanton slide of my cock between her legs is joined by the unmistakable sound of his fist around his cock.

"Christ," she whispers, and her eyes widen and look to me for answers. *"Christ,* that—"

I do the only logical thing and bury myself home. Instantly, my balls ache with relief given by her heat and wetness and the sublime way that she stretches, and she suddenly has no more questions.

"Yes," she says in a chant repeatedly brokenly under her breath. "Yes, yes, yes—James—*baby*—"

I lean her back, press her flat once again, and return my attention to her breasts. "Tell him that." I bend one knee to lift onto the table so I can thrust into her both harder and faster as her breasts bounce in my face. "Give him a taste. Tell him how wet he makes you. Tell him how you think about him while I give it to you any way you want it—and he knows how you want it, because I've told him. He knows all your favorite things, and I know you want to show them to him. *Fuck*, I want that too."

Her eyes squeeze shut and her pussy spasms, promising a swift conclusion for her—and for me too, probably, since her orgasm usually ends me. "You're too good to me," she says, the words whimpered. She reaches up above her head and clutches the edge of the table, and it lifts her breasts higher still. "I can't believe you'd—"

"I want to make you come—and, god, I want him there too. If having him there would get you off—"

"It would," she says, like she just fucking *knows*, and she wraps her legs around my waist to squeeze me even tighter. "Even just *thinking* about it—"

I tug her nipple between my teeth, tilt her hips higher, and say a quick, desperate prayer that the effect it all has on her won't take me apart before it does her. "Tomorrow. Do it for me tomorrow. Ask him if he's sick of fucking his hand and pretending it's you. Show him your pretty pussy if you want to, but—he doesn't touch it unless I'm there to watch."

Her arms tense, pulling soft skin taut, and the same tightness follows into her stomach and then into her legs. *"There,"* she says, and I lean down into her and clutch the table between her hands for better leverage. My panting breaths form condensation against her chest. "There—there—*fuck*—" She comes with her lip held between her teeth to stifle her cry as her pussy spasms around my twitching cock. Still gripping and hips grinding, her arms fall to my back, gather me closer still, and egg me to get my own end with every bit of the same ferocity that she'd chased her own. "God, I love you," she says breathlessly, and that's nearly enough. Her nails dig into my back and her heels into my ass, and she flexes ruthlessly around me, begging me to spill. "I love you so much, but—Jesus, baby, I might love your cock *more*—"

I lose it, emptying inside her with a mind-altering intensity that still makes the world spin. It feels that way, at least, as she clenches one final time, dragging every last sound from my throat and drop from my cock.

Afterwards, I might never move again, and, although my blood continues to pound in my ears, I still hear it: the latch of the door clicking softly, as if someone else has finished as well.

She runs her fingers through my hair, and her chest hums softly when her nails draw a shiver across my back. "I'm going to want you again as soon as you can," she says. "Slowly, though. I want to ride you, but I want you to beg me for it first."

My cock jerks, the pressure in my balls torn somewhere between pain and pleasure at the very thought, and I kiss her slowly, luxuriantly, savoring the taste of her mouth and the twisting of her fingers in my hair. "Fifteen minutes," I tell her, and her teeth gently tease my lower lip. I sigh, exhausted, sated, and pleased beyond measure. "Ten if you suck my cock."

Her mouth curves against mine. "Done."

I pull out of her eventually, clean where I spill out onto her thighs with a quick swipe of my discarded shirt, and right my shorts as she fixes her dress and then retrieves disinfecting wipes from underneath the sink to wipe the tabletop down. "Luke said," she reminds me when she hears my snort, and she looks like a fantasy I've probably had before, with her hair mussed and the straps of her dress once again sliding down her arms as she bends across the table to scrub away where one of us—or both of us—has left a streak of glistening wetness across the glass top.

"And you'll do anything Luke says?"

The glance under her eyelashes comes out coy, and with far less guilt than I would have expected even half an hour earlier. "Only if you're there."

Fuck, it's not even going to take me ten minutes to get hard again.

She heads upstairs first, leaving me to kill the lights in her wake, and only after darkness falls do I hesitate outside Luke's door. The decision comes to me in a split second, an idea sparked and then quickly followed through. Pulling Millie's panties from my pocket, I loop the bit of lace over the handle of his door. The dampness of her arousal clings to the fabric and transfers to my fingers. With heat twisting in my stomach, I lift a fist to knock.

I'm already halfway up the stairs before his door slowly squeals open upon its hinges, but I still hear Luke's swift inhalation of breath when he finds the gift I've left him. He follows it with a sharp, instantaneous curse.

Tomorrow, then. It will happen tomorrow, *finally*, without a doubt.

CHAPTER 3

LUKE

I sleep maybe a wink, but not much more than that. It's hard to sleep when I'm constantly, well, *hard*, and the siren's song of Millie's panties calls to me endlessly, followed by a heavy dose of guilt every time I come with them clutched in my hand or wrapped around my cock.

Jesus, I don't *want* to want her. I never have. James has had her from before I'd even known she'd existed, way back when she was just a story of some faceless woman he'd lusted after in his lit class that he had talked about incessantly. I'd mocked him for it then, amused at the sudden change in my best friend that had transformed him from my best wingman and partner in crime to a devoted sap whose cock had sudden loyalty to a woman he'd never even kissed.

But then I'd met her, and then I'd understood. And now—

She never leaves my mind, or close to it. She's just constantly *there*, hovering somewhere behind every thought, every memory, every fantasy, her full mouth smiling and her hair curling wildly and her lush body barely concealed behind the shortest of dresses or tightest of blouses or—in recent days—the tiniest of bikinis. The latter has officially done me in the most, shutting off all the synapses in my brain with hardly more than a single glance at her, and god help me when she looks back. Mischief sparkles in her eyes, promising me things beyond my filthiest of fantasies, and *that*? That says a lot, because I've surely devoted more hours to stroking my cock to the thought of her than every other woman in the world combined. James has all but made sure of it, the bastard, by telling me time and time again about the impossible beauty of her body and the perfect suction of her mouth and the unreal tightness of her pussy. After years of such tales, it had already seemed purposeful, but after their performance last night? After listening to him probe her to admit that she wants me; after watching him fuck her vigorously atop the dining room table; after seeing him look towards my bedroom door more than once with dark purpose, as if egging me on, goading me, and all but telling me to enjoy the sights and sounds of her along with him?

Well, I'd certainly known then exactly what he wants to happen—what they *both* want to happen, to my shock and surprise and utter, impossible joy—and her wet panties on my doorknob had really only sweetened an impossibly sweet deal.

"You look like shit," he says the next morning when I emerge from my bedroom to find him eating cereal at the counter. He stands alone and messy-haired and grinning like the most satisfied man on earth.

Millie tends to have that effect on him, and I've never stopped coveting it for myself. That hunger, already ravenous, has only intensified overnight. It gnaws painfully at the pit of my stomach.

"I didn't sleep," I tell him, and he smirks as he chews.
"Why's that?"
"You know why."
"Do I?"

The urge to throw something at him, something large and heavy, rears its ugly head. "Fuck off. You knew what you were doing, putting those on my door. That was—"

"Did you put them to good use?"

"They're a fucking biohazard at this point."

He laughs, the dick, and so hard that his head flies back and he nearly chokes on his Cheerios. "Tell her that. She'll love it."

Hell, she might, given the breathless longing she'd evidenced when he'd talked about stroking his own cock to the thought of her.

No, not the thought of her. The thought of *us*, the three of us.

My poor, abused cock stirs at the very memory and all that it seems to promise for the future. I drop my elbows onto the countertop and press my face into my hands, trying to force the thought of *anything* to the forefront of my brain except the way her breasts had heaved as she'd stretched out across the table with her legs first spread wide for James' tongue and then clenched tight around his waist.

I hadn't even seen much of her, not as much as I'd wanted to see, thanks to an improper angle and the desire to not get caught. Still, it hadn't mattered. I'd seen enough of her to know that the reality of her body had somehow surpassed the hundreds of ways I'd imagined her undressed, and—

Women like that don't exist, or maybe *shouldn't* exist, especially not when they're connected to best friends.

"You should take a nap this afternoon," James adds, the suggestion casually given. "I'll take the others on a beer run or something, but maybe Millie will stay behind and keep you company."

My chin snaps up to find him watching me as he tips his bowl back to drain the last of his milk. "I—"

He stops me from having to figure out precisely what to

say. "Just remember what I said last night. You can't touch her until I'm there. Still, I'm sure you two can figure something out. I'm sure she'll be happy to show you what she'd like you to do to her, if nothing else."

The thought of Millie on my bed—or, hell, on the counter or the table or the couch or one of the lounges outside or *anywhere,* really—with her golden legs spread and her slender fingers plundering her pussy, is enough to make me stiffen.

Everywhere.

It's also enough to make me overlook what will later strike me: that James has just openly acknowledged that I had seen them together the night before, that I'd witnessed the entire episode from beginning to end, and that I know that they both want to share her with me.

"You should probably go jerk it one last time," James advises. He deposits his bowl in the sink and reaches for the coffee pot. He pours himself a cup and then fills a second, which he passes to me. "If you don't, you'll need to after you see what she's wearing today."

I don't heed his advice, mostly to avoid giving him the satisfaction. It comes back to bite me in the ass—or perhaps the cock—when Millie flounces down the stairs ten minutes later wearing a devastating cherry-red bikini. A gauzy white sarong hangs loosely off her waist, more transparent than opaque, and I nearly choke on my coffee when she turns to reveal the complete bareness of her round ass with only a thin strip of a thong covering between her cheeks.

Covering. The very notion is laughable.

James casts me a knowing look with unspoken laughter dominating his features, and he sets out to rub my face in my desire all day.

With clouds hanging in the sky, we opt for the house's private pool over the beach, and he sets up shop beside her, his lounge pulled so close to hers that they nearly overlap. He keeps one hand on her at all times when out of the water and in the sun, his fingers stroking her leg or winding in her hair or trailing along the flat plane of her stomach. She enters the pool more rarely than he or I do, but I swear the world stops every time she emerges. Water slides down the elegant length of her neck, swells over the delicious mounds of her breasts, cascades towards the scrap of fabric covering her pussy, rolls over her shapely ass, drips down her legs. The desire to lick every last drop from her skin swells so strong that I spend the majority of my time either in the water or on my stomach with my erection throbbing with constant, frustrating pressure in the waistline of my trunks.

James has his own problems containing himself, although he has much more freedom to act than I do. When she stretches out on her stomach to sun her back and unties the flimsy strings of her top with nimble fingers, I can almost *feel* his own desire ratchet up higher. He rolls onto his side immediately, his hand reaching to aid hers in clearing the bothersome ties from her skin, and then his chest heaves with a sigh as he trails a caress down her spine towards the slender waistband of the thong slung low around her hips. He brushes there, his smile instant when her spine curves in an arch so sinful that I have to literally bite my tongue to hold back my reaction, and then he leans forward to press a kiss to hear ear. His mouth remains there, his lips curving as he whispers, and her cheek turned towards him quickly flushes a sweet, pretty pink.

"They're getting out of hand," Kyle says by my side, his eyes rolled skyward. "I think he gets off on reminding the rest of us that we're not getting laid."

"Cassie and Annette are available," I tell him, those same words James had spoken to me in the ocean the day before.

Unlike me, it clearly gives Kyle pause. His eyes flit towards where Cassie lays stretched out on her back, her body a dangerous map of deep curves, and then to Annette, whose petite, compact frame promises otherworldly tightness. After a moment, his gaze returns to Cassie, and it stays there. "Maybe with Cass," he says. "If Aaron doesn't get there first."

Try it at the same time, I nearly suggest, but I don't. I haven't even tried it with James and Millie yet—*yet,* my brain repeats, clearly indicating that I've already made my mind up that it will happen—so I can't go around touting the virtues of two men sharing the same woman.

And yet—

I'm already almost positive that it's for me and that I'll love it wholeheartedly, and not just fucking Millie's brains out like I've imagined for years. The thought of James there too—watching me pleasure her and pleasuring her in turn, once again egging on my desire, telling her what to do, telling *me* what to do—has been a part of my fantasies for far longer than I'll admit even to myself.

Perhaps an hour later, after I can take it no longer, I strike.

I've never been able to stay away from her for long, even when I've known I should. My body simply calls for hers outside of my control, and I have myself lifted out of the water, my mind already solidly beside her, before James calls out from behind me where he lounges with Grant and Bryan in the shallow end of the pool. "Go check if Millie's awake, will you?" he asks, and—

He's my best friend for many reasons, and has been for most of our lives. Still, I've rarely appreciated his friendship more than I do when he offers excuses to let me near her—not to mention his absurd, whole-hearted *acceptance* of it.

She isn't asleep, and she tugs her coverup off her face when I stand over her, dripping water from my body onto the golden skin of her back and ass and legs. "Stop it!" she protests, laughing, and she squirms both deliciously and also as if she has no idea just how damn delectable she looks. "God, you're all wet—"

"And you're not?" I ask, the question dropped low as I throw myself onto James' vacant chair. James' acceptance or not, it still feels wrong to ask her something like that, but...I like it. I've always liked it, all of it, including the guilt and the shame and the forbidden nature of it all.

She arches an eyebrow, and warmth gathers again in her cheeks. Her blush and her bared body contrast beautifully, a juxtaposition of innocence and sin all at once, and I roll immediately onto my stomach to copy her supine pose. The mere scent of her tanning oil, coconut and slick and sweet, is enough to send me from half-hard to fully erect in seconds. "I'm not going to answer that," she says, her voice as quiet as mine, and that? That's enough of an answer for me.

"Davidson—" Her last name falls easily from my mouth in the same way I've addressed her from the moment she'd first slipped her hand into mine and introduced herself at a party in the weeks before James had manned up enough to ask her out. Her nose crinkles a little as she smiles, and I'm close enough that I could count the freckles that the sun has blossomed there. "You look fucking *lethal* in that suit."

That, combined with my earlier question, is one of the more forward things I've ever said to her, especially while sober. After a few drinks, outward expressions of my attraction are almost impossible to stifle. Yet sober? In the bright sunshine of day, so close to our friends—and her boyfriend and my best friend—that they could certainly overhear us if we raised our voices just a bit? I've never said anything quite like it, and it shows in her reaction.

Her breath catches and holds in the slender column of her throat. I wait for guilt to flash across her pretty features, as it sometimes does when I make her laugh too hard, or we flirt a little too openly, or she catches my eyes on her chest or her ass, or I find hers lingering on the lean muscles of my stomach.

It doesn't come. It seems like some corner has turned in her mind, a corner that promises something in the very near future that I desperately covet—and, *fuck*, like I'm not hard enough.

"James picked it out," she says softly. Her fingers paint gentle strokes on her towel beside her head, and, even pressed flat into the lounge, I can see her breasts swell as she takes a deep breath. "Do you want to know what he said the first time he saw me in it?"

"Desperately."

She laughs again—lower, throatier—like she thinks I joke, although I don't. "He said, 'Luke's going to lose his fucking mind when he sees your ass. He'll blow his load right in his trunks.'"

I can't swallow the sound that escapes my mouth, a faint groan that comes in time to the throbbing of my cock. Just the sight of her lips forming the word 'load,' a load that I'm definitely going to need to release sooner than later, tempts me further. Again, her breath catches, and the heat in her cheeks increases and spreads down to the soft hollow of her throat. "He knows me well. I—fuck, I *love* your ass. I always have."

There. *That's* the most forward thing I've ever said to her —and the bluntest too—and there's no taking it back, although the desire to do so spikes for one brief, anxious moment.

Maybe it's too much. Maybe I've misread the situation somehow, although I have no idea how. Maybe—

She obliterates those doubts in one fell swoop. "Is that how you'd want me, then?" she asks. "From behind and with my ass in the air, like James talked about last night?"

My brain fucking *explodes*.

I reach for her without thinking, and my hand gets as far as the damp curls pinned atop her head. I've touched her hair before, of course, and countless times, but never with such purpose. I crush it between my fingers, determined to bring her mouth to mine until I can no longer breathe, and then to maybe shove it down to take care of my throbbing cock.

She stops me with nothing more than a sharp look. "Not here."

It should infuriate me, the stoppage of such an act, but it doesn't. If anything, the guarantee it imparts—not here, but *somewhere*, which is beyond what I'd ever hoped I'd get from her even twenty-four hours earlier—only excites me further. Still, I swear, the pressure of the word hot on my tongue, and she whimpers a little in response—actually *whimpers*, that same sound James had pulled from her the night before with supreme ease, and my hips nearly respond by flexing into the lounge on instinct. *"Where?"* I demand, and it takes conscious effort to unwind my fingers from her hair. "Davidson, I'm seriously about to—"

"I love when you call me that." It comes out all in a rush, like a floodgate has opened inside her. Her legs tighten against one another and squeeze, constricting the muscles of her ass as if she tries to relieve some pressure of her own. I stare, transfixed, as she continues. "You're the only one who does, and—god, it makes me wet every time you say it. James has—he sometimes calls me that while we're fucking, when he's eating me out or giving it to me really hard, because he knows it makes me come every time."

"That—oh, fuck him. *Fuck* him." The thoughts escape unbidden, and, when I glance back to her face, she has her lower lip tugged between her teeth as she fights the most incredible combination of arousal and laughter that I've ever seen. "He's *using my lines* to get you off?"

She swallows, and I've surely never seen a more beautiful sight in my life. "I've started to think of it as him conditioning my body to want you even more."

On second thought—

I have the world's greatest friend, full stop.

"Tie your top," I tell her. "We're going inside."

"Everyone will know we're—"

"I don't fucking *care*. I'm not asking you, Davidson." As promised, her legs squeeze again, and I can almost feel that same pressure of her thighs around my fingers, around my face, around my poor, weeping cock. "I'm *telling* you. We're going inside, and you're going to give me something to come to that isn't just—fuck, just the *thought* of you, or your soaking panties in my hand, or—"

She sits up suddenly—not fully, but she rises enough onto her elbows that I have sudden access to the glorious sight of the side of one full breast and the tiniest hint of areola.

"You—*what?*" Her eyes flare wide, more whites than irises. "You have—"

Realization strikes a heavy blow. "You didn't know."

"Didn't know *what?*"

Fuck.

I stumble over it all slightly, my brain tripped up from a severe lack of blood that has gathered below my waistline, and it comes out awkward and stilted. "Last night, after—you know—"

"Say it."

I can't tell if she asks in pleasure or fury or something in between, but I follow her instructions. "After James made sure I'd hear everything by fucking you four feet away from my bedroom door only seconds after I went inside, because then he knew I'd *have* to—"

She waits when I falter, and she passes a hand over her hair. The motion lifts her breast, revealing a peaked, red nipple colored nearly as brilliant as the bikini top that lies uselessly beneath her. It's darker than I'd expected, and beautifully flushed and tight, and—

She catches the unavoidable pull of my eyes, but she doesn't cover herself. "Say it, Luke."

A shiver runs through me at my name on her lips, one strong enough to clench all the muscles of my stomach. "I listened. And then I opened up the door and I watched. And I came so hard in my hand that my legs almost gave out."

Her eyes flash encouragingly, but she says nothing.

"And then—" A breath comes difficultly. "There was a knock on my door, and I found—I found *your panties* dangling from my doorknob. And I—damn it, Davidson, I *lost* it."

She lays back down, the lowering of her body slow, and the tightness of her muscles remains. "How?" she asks, a single, honeyed word.

Arousal, then. Not fury at all. Her back rises quickly with her breaths, the tempo faster and picking up speed.

"How do you *think?*"

She licks her lips, her tongue slow and taunting and her eyes never leaving mine, just as she'd lovingly caressed every crevice of her spoon the night before as I'd stood close enough to her to feel the heat radiating from her skin. I feel that heat again, but tenfold. "Tell me," she says. "Tell me *everything.*"

This woman is going to kill me. There's no way around it.

Well, at least I'll die happy.

"They were still wet from you," I tell her, and she whimpers again, her legs shifting, squeezing, flexing, each movement minute and subtle but purposeful. "Fucking *soaked* from your pussy and James' tongue, and I wrapped them around my cock and imagined what it would feel like to hear you moan my name the way you moaned James'—"

"*God*, Luke," she breathes, giving me precisely what I want, and I nearly come right there.

"Get up!" Cassie's bright, peppy voice chirps, and suddenly she's right beside Millie's chair with a slinky black coverup already stretched across her body. "Come on. We're going on a beer run."

James appears too, with water dripping from his hair, and he grins down at me as he tugs his towel out from under my body. "You look like you're about to fall asleep out here, same as Mills."

I catch the thread, and it breaks frustration into a relief so strong that I nearly sweat with it. Quickly, I grasp his hint and run with it. "I could use it. I couldn't sleep last night."

Millie shifts beside me, her body rustling softly, and I try not to notice.

"You're going to be useless tonight, aren't you?" James rubs at his hair. "Whatever. Stay. Get your beauty rest so you don't pack it in early when we're drinking tonight. Babe, you coming?"

Oh, she'll be coming, alright.

Millie's pretty throat contracts as she swallows again. "I'll stay with Luke," she says, and I've never heard such incredible words in my entire life.

Around us, everyone else shuffles into shirts and coverups and flip-flops; each second they take is agony. "Yeah, alright," James agrees easily, and when Cassie wanders away to join Annette, he takes her spot at Millie's side. He bends over, kisses the flush of her exposed cheek, and then lingers beside her ear as he strokes a strong, commanding hand over her ass. He squeezes and she moans, a faint sound that hits my ears with a blow that feels physical. "Be good for Luke," he says lowly, and he brushes a second kiss against her temple. "Put him out of his misery, will you? Roll over and show him your pretty tits. He can't take his eyes off them."

He squeezes again, harder, and his fingertips dip heavily into her firm cheek. "Let him come on them if he wants—and he'll want to, babe, you should see his face when I tell him about finishing there—but—"

"*James—*" she whispers fiercely, but it comes out as more of a plea than anything else.

I'm incapable of forming my own words, or truly even my own thoughts. My mind has shut down entirely, a complete victim to the wants and whims of my cock.

James ignores her. "The thong stays on," he continues smoothly. "And you don't touch each other. Make him wait for it, okay? I want to be there when it happens." He glances to me and winks, his expression pleasure personified. "Get her warmed up for tonight. We'll give her the time of her life."

At that, my tongue finally works. "Look at her. She's already warmed up."

"Like you're not?" Millie shoots back. "Both of you? There's no way you're not—"

"Stay," I urge James. "Send the others. Let's give her what she wants now."

He shakes his head easily. "Nah. I want to take my time with her tonight. I don't want to rush it under a time limit of them coming back. Besides, she likes the wait. She gets off on it."

She gives a soft, breathy whine, something that spikes my pulse even further. "Baby—"

"James!" Grant calls. "Let's go!"

It's just in time, by the look of it. James' expression darkens, his eyes suddenly sharp at the single use of the endearment, and he no longer looks like a man who had had his fill of her the night before. Suddenly, he's clearly *starving* for her, his appetite only increasing mine, and—

"Later." He kisses her one final time, this one falling upon her mouth. She winds her fingers into the back of his hair, tugs him closer to bite gently at his lip, and I'm near enough to hear her tongue stroke his. *"Later, babe, I promise,"* he says a second time, the words pressed against her mouth. He sounds resolute, although that tenacity wavers briefly when she tugs at his hair. "Wait until we leave. Count to ten, and then use your fingers to show him how quickly you can come when you're worked up like this."

"James," I say after he stands, turns, and takes a few strides away. "You—"

Fuck, what is there I can say to sum up everything that courses through me? How can I properly thank him for this blatant trust and this sharing of the only person I've ever seen him truly covet, and then cherish, and then love, and then guard so jealously that it has become something of a running joke among our friends? For him to want to be there to watch me with her is one thing—a thing I understand all too well, having watched her with him the night before—but to trust me alone with her with nothing more than a few casual warnings that seem meant more to titillate than dissuade? What the hell did I do in a past life to deserve that level of trust and this sort of reward?

"You're the best," I tell him, and it falls woefully short.

Yet he makes it appear otherwise. He laughs, his grin broad, and waves a hand before he strides away. "And don't forget it!" he calls over one shoulder, and he follows behind the others as they traipse out the side gate.

In comparison to the laughter and raised voices and splashing that had continued all day, the backyard falls silent.

"Count to ten," Millie tells me, and I immediately regret looking at her. She has her towel clutched in both hands, her eyes brim with anticipation, and her ass bears the faint red marks of James' fingers. The latter glows like a blueprint meant to guide my touch, and, with my heart pounding in my mouth, I follow it. I skate my fingertips across her ass for the first time, trailing a caress over one smooth cheek, and she moans again, just as she had for James. *"Luke—"* My name comes out tightly from her throat, full of heated need, and that's enough. That's *more* than enough.

I kiss her, a crushed meeting of lips quickly followed by tongues, and she swallows my low sound of relief. Her mouth opens under mine, hot and eager, and her hands follow, gripping the tight muscles of my shoulders to pull me closer. Her nails dig into my flesh, ripping a growl from my chest, and I turn her forcefully, both hands gripping her shapely hips to all but throw her onto her back. She gasps, and I swallow that sound as her tongue twists skillfully against mine, her lips soft and her teeth a faint promise of roughness to come. Without pause, I slide onto her lounge and in between her waiting legs, and then lean down to hover over her fully.

"*Years*, Davidson," I say against the kiss, the words dark, uneven, unlike me. I thrust forcefully against her pussy, the single motion so good that it draws me up short, and my mouth breaks inelegantly from hers. "I've wanted you for *years*, felt so fucking guilty over it that it's kept me up at night, dreamt about—"

"Me too, me too," she says hurriedly, her breath warm against my face. Her nails trace down my back, and when she wraps her legs around my waist, drawing my cock solidly against her, I groan from relief. "God, you've driven me crazy —and *James* has driven me crazy, telling me that you wanted me too and that it's okay and not to feel bad, but—"

"How long? How long has he been—?"

"I don't even know—*forever*, it's felt like, but—"

I muster the control to open my eyes, take in her wonderfully flushed face, glance at the way it spreads down onto her throat, and feel my insides seize.

It escapes before I can stop it. "Fuck, you're beautiful." I'm captivated by the perfect fullness of her breasts; by the rosy nipples just inches from my chest; by the mere rise and fall of her breath, which is somehow the most erotic thing I've seen in almost twenty-six years of life. "Oh, what the *fuck,* Davidson. It's not fucking *fair*—"

She laughs, the sound breathless and a little wild, and her chest darkens with color too. Freckles have also sprouted there, and, combined with her flush, they look like a delicate chain of stars that have gathered at sunset.

Jesus. She's turned me into an insurmountable sap without even letting me inside her—just like she had years ago with James. What the fuck is this woman's *deal?*

It doesn't matter, truly. Her hips lift, rocking a slow, smooth circle against my cock, and even just *that,* friction through clothes that hasn't done much for me since high school, is better than I've ever dreamed. If she somehow hadn't lived up to all my expectations and my fantasies—if kissing her had fallen flat, or if her body didn't feel like heaven against mine, or if her eyes didn't stare up at me so captivatingly—I could maybe back out.

But now? Now that she's surpassed my every expectation and then some? Jesus, I'm about to fall so far into this woman that I might never find my way out.

"Luke—" she says, my name the prettiest of pleas, and then she drags me back down to her mouth to die happily.

I kiss her in every way I can imagine, every way I've dreamt and ruminated over—hot and desperately like I feel for her constantly; slowly, languidly, almost lazily, as I'm sure James often couples with her after a long night of sex; lightly and teasingly to make her whimper and chase down my lips. She coaxes me wordlessly, perhaps without even knowing she does it, as she releases a veritable symphony of delighted sighs and gentle moans and subdued whimpers into my open mouth. I drink them all in. I drink *her* in—the sugary taste of her mouth from whatever fruity drink she's just finished, the salty slickness of her sweat when I bend to suck at her neck, the fragrant oil of her chest as I trace the contours of her breasts with my tongue. She directs me not just with her hands, which hold me in place on particularly sensitive spots on her neck, but unconsciously too, as I feel every flex and clench of her pussy against my cock even through her suit and mine.

"*Jesus*, Davidson—" I groan against her nipple, and her muscles tighten beautifully. "Can I take my cock out? I want —fuck, I want *inside* you, but—that'll do for now. Can I—"

"*Yes*," she says, the single word hungry, voracious, as greedy as her fingers in my hair. "God, I wish I could touch you—"

"Later," I say, an unintentional echo of James' earlier promise. Her pussy clenches again, as if she hears it herself, and my brain picks it up then. *"Later,"* I repeat, a careful experiment, and she gives another panting whimper that promises me the world. "I have so many plans for you, but not until—"

"Tell me. Tell me your plans." She releases me and allows me to sit up and clear just enough space to wrap my hand around my cock, and she sucks her plump lower lip between her teeth when I bring it over the top of my trunks. "Oh, wait —" Her hand flies out, wrapping around my wrist, and her fingers close over top of my hand mere inches from my cock. At the squeezing behest of her fingers, I stroke up, over the swollen tip, and smear precum back down my length in a familiar, often-tread path. "Will you—I want to watch you. I want to see you—"

I swear, the sound torn somewhere between frustration and pleasure, which just about sums up the sight of her breathless and needy and spread wide without the ability to do a thing about it. "I'm—*god*, Millie—" I rarely call her that, and it spurs something new in her, something that leads her to sit up and kiss me like she can hardly stand another second of separation. I reach for her hair, grip the length in one tight hand, and thrust into my fist again. "I'm fucking *tired* of doing it myself. I want—"

"I know," she says, and she guides my hand faster, halting my words like water from a tap abruptly closed. Her lips ghost across my cheek, and she nuzzles just underneath my ear, her breath quick. "But—James has talked about it so much, about how he knows you get off to me, and I—"

"I *do*. I've practically rubbed my cock raw thinking about you, and for *years*—"

She laughs, and, despite it all, I'm so conditioned to the sound that I smile with her. "*Please*, Luke?" she says, her tongue flicking against my earlobe, and—

I'm fucked. I'm immediately so fucked, because I know in a heartbeat that I'll do whatever she asks in order to get her to say my name again in just that way.

I bring her mouth closer to my neck and she takes the hint. She skims her lips across the shell of my ear and nips dangerously just below. "What's in it for me?" I ask.

I can hear her smile, and she brings her free hand up to wrap around my neck. Her breasts press against my chest, soft and full and perfect. "You can come on my tits."

I swallow a quick agreement. "What else?"

She laughs again, the sound gentle. "I'll touch myself for you."

"*Fuck*, Davidson—"

Her tongue dances down, swirls against my collarbone, and sends a whole new—but also very old—fantasy into my head of the magic she could surely create with that clever tongue on my cock. "And you can have me however you want me later, as long as James is okay with it."

Without a doubt, it's the best deal I've ever heard in my life.

A world of possibilities explode inside my mind. Instantly, I recall all the ways I've thought about fucking her —hard and fast and desperate, slow and almost tender, my body pinned down and entirely at her mercy, her stretched out and eager to do whatever I please. I think about her on her knees, practically gagging on my cock; her riding me backwards so I can watch her ass move; her pussy pressed onto my mouth as her hips work over top of my face, my tongue at the service of her needs; her bent over the edge of a bed or a couch or a counter or anywhere, really, so I can pound into her with years of pent-up lust. I tighten my grip on my cock, my hips rocking, the tip repeatedly brushing against the sun-drenched skin of her stomach. "Deal. Just— deal. Lay back and fuck your fingers for me."

She follows my instructions to the letter. When she pulls her mouth from my overheated skin, a flash of disappointment strikes my chest, but it vanishes altogether as she stretches out on her back again. Her pert nipples are slick from the prior attention of my tongue, her flat stomach heaves with panting breaths, and her long legs spread wide and then wider still as her delicate hand winds down her body, tracing over the curve of her breast and then her hip before coming to rest just above the low line of her thong. Her fingers trace along the top, stroking a scintillating path, and her forehead crinkles as if the motion torments her as deeply as it does me. "You're so hot," she says, and her legs spread a little wider as she dips her index finger into the front of her thong. Her eyes trace my face, my chest, my stomach, and come to rest where I jerk my cock with the potential for something far more rewarding than anything I've achieved of late. "*So* hot. It's—god, it's your smile and your laugh and your arms and your chest and your stomach and—just *all* of you. I've dreamt about dragging my tongue over the lines of your abs and hips for *years*."

My chest swells with unmistakable pride, a pride that goes straight to the growing pulse in my balls. "You can," I tell her, and her middle finger joins her index in sliding lower into her bottoms. Soon, her whole hand follows; through the thin fabric, I can see her fingers move, flexing as she does something—perhaps some swirl to her clit, or a swipe to her opening, or a curving insertion into her pussy—that makes her moan. "After I fuck you, I'll give you as long as you want to do anything you want to me—but only after we fuck. There's no way—*no* way—that your mouth is getting anywhere near my cock without you actually sucking it, and—I won't make it inside you if that happens. I'll end up blowing in your perfect mouth, and—"

"*Yes,*" she whimpers softly, and her eyes close as she does something else between her legs—something I'd *sell my soul* to see—that makes her head tip back. "I want to taste you so bad. I—here, here—" She sounds panicked, almost, as her free hand reaches for the wrist that furiously chokes my cock. With the barest modicum of pressure, she pulls my hand away, and—

I realize what she means to do mere seconds before she does it. With eyes locked in mine, she brings my hand up to her mouth. Her tongue darts out from between parted lips, and she licks a slow, sensual stripe up my palm, collecting the shiny precum spread there. As her tongue travels, she moans, the sound low and sweet, like the taste of me brings her unspeakable pleasure, and that shows in the desperate work of her hand beneath her bottoms. Her fingers move in quick, tight circles, circles I can't see but also can, circles that I know will haunt my every moment—waking and sleeping—until I see them acted out with no barrier in place. Her tongue swirls, gathering every last drop from the pad of my thumb and then the length of my fingertips. Finally, just as I recognize that I'm swearing repeatedly through lips I cannot feel, she sucks two of my fingers in between her wonderfully swollen lips. She takes them deep, her cheeks hollowing and her tongue twisting so gloriously that I can almost feel it around my pulsing length.

"*Fuck,*" I hear myself say, and I don't think. I yank her fingers from beneath her thong, gather the wrist along with her other one, and use my free hand to slam them above her head. She whimpers around my fingers, the tight pressure of her mouth increasing further, and I thrust my cock against her pussy, grind a slow circle against her pelvis, and thrust again. "Fuck, fuck, *fuck,* you're—fuck yes, Davidson, keep—"

It all follows along those lines, an incomprehensible stream of pleasure and frustration and pleas, and her eyes look more beautiful than I've ever seen as they trace the slip of each word from my lips. She sucks my fingers deep with a greedy sound that rips at my soul, spins her tongue, gives a breathy request as I draw them back out, and moans when I drive them again past her lips. My hips rock in tandem with the destructive motions of her mouth, my cock leaking further in response to the damp patch that grows against her pussy, and it would be easy, *so* easy, to slip the scanty fabric aside and plow into her. Not only that, but she'd surely welcome it with a cry of relief from her throat. She wants it bad, wants *me* bad, and holding back from giving her everything she needs is simultaneously the most intoxicating and torturous thing I've ever experienced.

"I can't *wait* to fuck your mouth," I tell her, and she wraps her legs around my waist once again, like a wordless plea to continue. "James swears there's nothing like it on earth, except—fuck, except for your pussy, and I—that's what I want tonight. I want you waiting for me with your ass in the air while you use James' cock to show me all the things he's bragged that you can do with your mouth."

It's precisely what he'd said he'd wanted the night before, the fact of which doesn't escape me. Again, I'm not who first had the idea of the three of us together, but we've apparently fallen into a sort of feedback loop where one person's thoughts and desires influence the other's, and—well, I'm not exactly mad. It's quite possibly the hottest thing that's ever happened to me.

Her legs squeeze my hips, and her pussy follows suit, like she tries to draw me inside her even with a barrier in place. "God—" she says, a word formed around my fingers, and I pull them clear of her mouth, lift my hand up to where I pin her wrists, and lean down further. "Oh, he's going to *love* that."

Apparently, just based on the starry look in her eyes and the growing tautness of her body, this is the hottest thing to ever happen to her too.

I kiss her lips, her chin, her jaw, her neck, pulling fresh gasps from her. "And when he gets back—" I locate a spot on her neck, some inconsequential slip of skin that looks no different from the rest of her, but that makes her pussy spasm anew. "You're going to tell him I said that, so *he* can fucking wait for a while."

She laughs, almost certainly at the bitter frustration that I hardly even mean, and her legs tighten to a proper stranglehold around my waist. "Good," she says, and her wrists tense under my hands as her fingers clench suddenly. "Good, he —*oh*. Oh, *Christ,* Luke—"

I hear it, the beginning of the end in her voice, and the heaviness in my balls increases tenfold. "Come," I tell her, and she squirms promisingly underneath me. I tug my face out from her neck and catch the impossibly beautiful flush of her cheeks and the bite of her lip and the furrow of her brow over closed eyes. I drag my hips in another quick circle, and then another, and then another. *"Come,* Davidson, so I can blow on your tits. I'm fucking—I'm *aching,* babe, and you feel so—"

Her eyes snap open. Only later, once I've regained some semblance of sanity, will I remember that only James calls her "babe,' and often.

It proves her undoing.

She comes with a throaty noise held back with her teeth, and, as she contracts mercilessly against my cock, I release her wrists so I can tug her lip free and really hear her. "Oh—*oh,"* she says, both gasped, and her back arches to press her breasts against me fully. "Luke—Luke—*god,* Luke—"

It's enough to send me. Again, it's *more* than enough, and I break out from between her clenched legs and straddle her waist instead, one hand back around my pulsing cock and the other dropped low to grasp my balls. It only takes a few erratic tugs. I come onto her waiting breasts, and she watches it all. Instantly, she swipes a thumb across the seed spilt over one taut nipple. Still panting, she slips her dripping thumb into her mouth, and—

I'd groaned in release before, but I fairly bellow as another splash of cum jerks free. The intensity is enough to nearly make me collapse, and I'm forced to release my balls so I can catch myself. I lean down towards her, my hand pressed to the lounge above her head, as I chase the last traces of the greatest release I've ever felt.

I tell her that when my throat finally works again—or try to, at least. "Holy shit," I say, the second word more groaned than spoken. "Holy *shit,* you're—what the fuck did you just *do* to me?"

She laughs that pretty little Millie laugh, one that she's given to my jokes for years, although I'm certain I'll never hear it the same way again. She releases her thumb from her mouths and swipes her tongue across her lips for good measure, and my cock twitches in response. "What did *you* just do to *me?*" she counters, and it is, without a doubt, the best stroke my ego has ever received.

I kiss her, lower myself onto her entirely, and hear the tiny noise of protest she gives when cum transfers to my chest. "Leave it," I tell her, skimming fingers down the sides of her torso. She wiggles deliciously in response. "It doesn't bother me. It's *my* cum, after all, and it looks fucking perfect on you."

She laughs again, and this time I join, our breaths mingling as she opens her mouth to the slow pressure of my tongue. I taste myself on her, salty not unlike the sweat from her neck, and she winds her arms around me as if she intends to hold me to her for a good, long while.

I'll give her that. I'll give her every moment I can until the others return, and then I know I'll be counting the seconds—perhaps literally—until James and I take her for ourselves tonight.

CHAPTER 4

MILLIE

It takes James several hours to make it happen, hours we spend chatting and laughing and drinking with our friends, but he gets me alone and corners me in the end.

"Tell me everything," he demands, his voice a growl, as he shoves my back up against the wall near the downstairs hall bathroom. Instantly, he has himself entirely in my space, our chest and stomachs and hips and thighs all touching, and he leans a forearm on either side of my head to fairly box me in. He's foregone a shirt ever since our pool time, and his smooth skin radiates heat and the unique, piney scent of his body that I've come to crave. *"Everything*, babe. All of it. Leave nothing out."

I should still feel sated from the afternoon with Luke—not to mention the long night before with James—but my pussy starts to ache immediately.

Jesus, what have these two done to me? James has always had this sort of power to turn me on with hardly more than a glance, but there's usually some build to it. It's never this immediate, this all-encompassing, this *constant*, and—

Based on the way he speaks, the way he looks at me, the way he throbs against my stomach, he feels similarly.

"It was—" My voice breaks off as he bends to my neck, his lips moving slowly and his tongue sucking lightly. "Oh, god, James, it was good."

It hardly scratches the surface of anything that had happened between me and Luke—let alone explains a single thing that I'd felt, of which the word 'fireworks' hardly suffices—but James doesn't care. He groans, the sound reverberating across my skin, and those same fireworks explode again through every vein in my body.

"Yeah?" He drops an arm, loops if around my waist, and palms my ass through the thin, black linen of my dress. "Did you come for him?"

"Yes." I tug at his hair to pull his mouth towards my ear, and he groans again in response. "So hard I thought the neighbors might come running."

He freezes, his lips halting in a hot path behind my ear. "You stayed outside?"

I freeze in turn. "Yes." Is that displeasure that pulls his muscles tight?

It's not. *"Fuck*, that's hot," he says, his hips grinding against me, and my leg lifts on instinct. He drops his knees a little, hitches my leg up over one hip, and lines the length of his cock up against my waiting pussy in a dance we've practiced both in and out of clothes more times than I can count. "Anyone could have seen you out there, tits out, calling his name. Did you do that for him? Did you moan his name like you do for me?"

"Yes."

His hand slides slowly up the outside of my thigh, traveling from my knee at an excruciating pace. "Did he love it?"

"It's what made him come. And—" When my voice falters, his hand stills, waiting. "I touched myself for him. He couldn't see, because I left my bottoms on like you said, but—"

He chuckles, the sound like dark sin across my skin. "Good girl."

The praise does something devilish to my insides, twisting the inner workings of my stomach and lower still, and he feels it. He hears it catch my breath, too, and he halts the taunting trace of his lips against my ear to look at me.

"*Such* a good girl," he says, almost as if to test me, and my hips attempt to lift from the wall. He uses the hand on my ass to clutch me tighter, to hold me to him even more firmly, and he rocks against me with slow, smooth strokes. "You listened so well. Did he touch you?"

I swallow; it takes effort. "No. You told him not to."

He smiles, a slow grin that stretches across his strong, tanned jaw, and the sight pools further heat between my thighs. *Jesus,* he has no idea how beautiful he is. "I did. I just didn't know if he'd listen. You're very hard to resist. I don't know if I would have had it in me to stop from fucking your eager little pussy." His fingers skim higher, pause, and drop lower again in a wordless taunt. "Was it hard for him? Was he desperate for you?"

It feels arrogant to admit, but I know the answer well. The memory of the wild desire in Luke's amber eyes, the furious intensity of his words, the vigorous pounding of his body against mine—it's all too much to deny. "Yes. He told me he's wanted me for years."

If possible, James' grin widens further. "Did he, now?" He traces a slow circle with his thumb, a gentle shape painted as he gives my thigh a teasing squeeze. "He used to try to hide it, you know, but I could still tell. He always—"

Memory sparks, although from what, I don't know. "I can't believe you *put my panties* on his *door,*" I hiss, and his grin flickers long enough for a brief blip of doubt to creep across his face.

The hand on my ass slips away and migrates to my neck; his long fingers touch gently below my chin. He tips my face back, and his eyes search mine. "Are you mad?"

"Well—no, but—"

His expression clears. "I figured you wouldn't be. I mean, you knew he was watching us. After that, I thought we should throw the poor guy a bone."

He snorts with laughter, clearly pleased with his word-play, and I lift an eyebrow. "Is that what you're planning tonight? A *bone?*"

He strokes my chin lightly, and something shifts in his face. His dark eyes soften in the corners, and his smile tempers with it, transforming into something achingly sweet as he bends to brush his nose against mine. "That's what I'd like," he says, and he kisses me just once and very softly. "That's—I think you can tell that's what I'd like." As if to drive his point home, he gives a single, harder thrust and remains there with cock pressed tight against my pussy. "But I'll do whatever you want. I'm sure he will too. We'll move at whatever pace you decide."

Just like that, I could melt against the wall in an entirely different way.

"I love you," I tell him, and he kisses me again. His mouth continues to smile against mine. "I love you so much—"

He sighs, the sound soft, content. "Good. Good, because—I get crazier about you every day, I swear. And I'd *never*—" He pulls back suddenly, sharply, to look me directly in the eye. "I'd never share you with *anyone* else. Just Luke. You're—" He rocks again, slower, deliberately, maddeningly. "You're *mine*, Millie, but…you can be ours."

Ours.

The notion hits me with a jolt that feels physical, like a

dose of hot pleasure that slides down my throat. "And you'd —you're okay with that?" I ask, my pulse quickening even further until I'm nearly dizzy with it.

He takes my hand from his hair to slip it in the infinitesimal space he clears between our bodies, and he turns my palm towards his cock. My fingers close on instinct, cradling him through the slick fabric of his basketball shorts, and he drops his forehead to press against mine, a moan low in his throat. "What do you think?" he asks, throbbing into my hand. "Does it—*fuck*—does it feel like I'm okay with it?"

I stroke him slowly, drag my thumb across his tip, slide my hand back down to cup his balls. "Yes. *Yes.* God, baby—"

"Unfair," he grinds out, and his hand finally slips up my thigh towards my hip, where his fingers close.

Instantly, he freezes.

"Mills—" he says, a spike of thick disbelief coloring my nickname. "Are you seriously not wearing panties?"

My throat has lost my breath. "Yes. If you're going to give them away, I really don't see the point in even putting them on."

Laughter mixes with his low swear, and I catch a single glimpse of his expression, his teeth brilliant and his eyes longing, before he drags my mouth to his.

We kiss and we kiss and we kiss, with the weight of his body crushing mine in the most incredible way. His hand explores every inch of my thighs and hips and ass like it's all still new territory for him to discover and conquer, and, in return, my hand draws forth a wet patch from the tip of his cock. Eventually, he gives up, grabs my hand from his cock, and slams it onto the wall behind me in a near-perfect replication of Luke's earlier motion from the day. The memory of pleasures of the past mix with those had in the present, the thoughts swirling in time to his tongue against mine, and it's so good that I could nearly weep.

"*Fuck*, you're wet," he says, a throaty whisper had between his teeth. "You're going to be dripping down your thighs by the time we finally get you to bed."

We. God help me, because I might not make it there. I might collapse before then, simply too turned on to function.

"And I'm going to have to go change my shorts before then," he adds, a chuckle soft against my lips. "And soon, because—the thought of you with him—the noises you're making—the way you feel, Millie, *fuck*—I could lose it right here, and I don't want that. I want to wait until we're all together, and—I don't care if I get your mouth or your pussy. I'm happy with either. Let him pick where he wants to start."

It jogs some scrap of my memory, and I tug at his hair, lick at his lips, wrestle against the one hand he has pinned in an effort to get closer to him. "He told me—*god*, James—he told me to tell you what he wants tonight."

"Yeah?" When I open my eyes, I find him staring at me from the space of a few inches. His dark eyes gleam, more pupil than iris. "Go on, then. Tell me."

I'm closing in on the brink of it, of the desperate end that my swollen clit craves, and I know he can tell. He slows his hips, and he drags his cock deliberately against me in a thrust that tilts upwards from my opening to my clit. My eyes close again, my head tips back uselessly, and body lights on fire. "*Again.* Please—*please* do that again."

"Tell me what Luke said."

"He said—" I swallow, the sound loud in my ears, and he presses a kiss to the base of my throat. "He told me he wants it exactly like you said last night, where he takes me from behind while I show him how far I can swallow your cock down my throat."

His breath comes in sharp against my neck, and I shift

against him, desperate for some kind of friction. For a moment, just based on the way he squeezes my wrist, I'm almost certain he's about to give me precisely what I want. After all, he usually does.

Yet then he steps back, his body wrenched from outside of my grasp so suddenly that I stumble a little. He reaches out to steady me, one large hand hot over the fabric atop my hip, but he lets me go again quickly. "We're going to wait," he says, his tone brusque. He drags a hand over his face and continues speaking into his palm. "We're both going to wait, so don't you *dare* go into the bathroom and finish yourself off."

I can only stare. *"Me?* Yesterday, you're the one who—"

"I'll wait," he says, but when he glances down at the ruined front of his shorts, darkened significantly from both of us on separate sides of the fabric, he swears into his hand. "I—fuck, I'll wait, okay? I just—I want to watch Luke finish you off and know that I got you most of the way there."

Jesus, that's maybe the most incredible thing I've ever heard, and my thighs tremble with it.

It must show on my face, because his own expression darkens. "None of that," he warns, his eyes hot on my face. "None of that—that *look* you give, babe. It's not fair."

It slips from my mouth unintentionally in what must be a subconscious desire to strike. "Baby—"

He takes half a step forward, his weight leaning onto the ball of one foot, but thinks better of it. "None of that either, Millie, *fuck,*" he says, and the curse pulls something desperate from me, some form of whine that makes his jaw lock. Every muscle of his broad shoulders, of his toned chest, of his tight stomach, clenches beautifully. "Or that. You're—you're *killing* me, babe." He rubs his face again, and rougher than before. "Look, I'm going to go change, and you're going to go tell

Luke you're not wearing panties. At least then he'll fucking suffer like I am."

"If you get yourself off—"

"I won't, but you better not either. Be a good girl and wait for me, alright?"

Again, my legs quiver. *"That's* not fair. Don't call me—"

His hand remains stretched across his face, but I see his eyes crinkle with the smile it obscures. "We're going to have fun with that later," he promises, and, with that, he leaves me fairly panting against the wall.

It takes a while for my breath to return, for my stomach to uncoil, for my legs to steady. When I return to the main living area—somehow both a million miles away from the hall but also only a couple dozen feet—I find the party in the same high swing that I'd left it.

Almost immediately, Luke disengages from a conversation with Aaron and Kyle, and he joins me at my side when I go to grab a new drink from the fridge. Like James, he hasn't put on a shirt—like all of the guys, actually, although I can hardly even notice anyone else. The sun has turned his bronze skin darker still, and he glows in the fluorescent overhead light, his body flexing smoothly as he leans up against the counter. "You look a bit flushed," he says casually, quietly. "Deliciously flushed." He holds a dark bottle in his hand, and moisture clings to his lips after he takes a sip.

I'm not a beer drinker myself, but he could probably convert me.

"Aaron went to take a piss and said he couldn't use the hall bath because you were giving James a hand job right outside," he continues with his eyebrows high upon his forehead.

I pull a spiked seltzer from the fridge, and I don't even bother to check what kind. My fingers still shake a little as I crack the top. I know he notices, because his eyebrows slide higher still. "Through the clothes and not to completion, so it's only a mild exaggeration."

His mouth quirks in the corners with a suppressed smile. "Pretty good for Aaron."

I pull a hand through my hair, take a sip I don't taste, try to forget the dampness between my legs. "Isn't it?"

Yet he won't let me ignore the latter, because he shifts his beer from one hand to the other so he can press his fingers to the side of my neck. My pulse skitters recklessly underneath fingertips chilled from his drink, and that's enough. I shiver, a fresh wave of arousal coasting through my body, and his face sharpens expectantly. Suddenly, he looks at me just as he had earlier that day by the pool, with such all-encompassing thirst that I have to lean back against the fridge simply for support.

Things have turned a corner between us. He's looked at me like that on and off all night, no longer cloaking the desire he's apparently felt for years, and I wait for guilt to come.

It doesn't.

I guess that has turned a corner too, with doubt and guilt both chased away by the enthusiastic desire and enjoyment that both men have expressed at the thought of sharing me with each other.

"Your neck is a bit red," he says, softer still, and he licks his lips. I stare, transfixed, at the slow motion of his tongue and the promise of all it could do to me. "Tell me, Davidson...what did James do to you that has you worked up like this?"

I could drag it out, could stretch the explanation across several minutes of throaty, taunting words and all the longing looks I feel. Normally, I probably would. It's a game James and I have enjoyed with each other for years, and I'm sure Luke would like it too.

But I can't. James has pushed my nerves so far towards an end with no conclusion that I don't have the patience for it. "He wanted to know about this afternoon," I tell him, and he licks his lips again, the pace slower still.

"Did he now." He doesn't pose it as a question. "And what did you tell him?"

"I told him I came so hard I thought the neighbors might come running."

He laughs, his head rocking back with the force of it, and he shifts subtly on his feet. It turns his back to the rest of the house, and he focuses his attention solely on me. "I see why he has such a big head now," he says, his fingers still light on my neck. They warm slowly as he strokes, heating up with my skin. "Making you come could do that to anyone. I can't imagine what I'd be like after a few years of it. I probably wouldn't survive it, if I'm honest. I haven't even been inside you yet, but I'm already pretty sure I'd forget to eat or drink if I had uninterrupted access to you for a long period of time."

"Luke—" It flies from my mouth like a warning, one desperately put, and he picks it up eagerly.

"What?" His head tips, and his thumb slides over the hollow of my throat as he takes a swig of beer. "Seriously, what did James do to you? You look like you're about to come just from listening to me talk. I'm not complaining—again, my ego loves it, and I get why his is so big—but—"

My patience breaks. "He got me ten seconds away from climax and then told me I had to wait for you to finish me off while he watches."

He chokes on his drink.

It happens spectacularly, a true definition of a near-perfect spit take, although he stifles his drink from spewing towards me at the last moment. He presses a harsh cough into his fist, his face red, his eyes watering, his throat working overtime, and—

Somehow, it helps to watch him visibly struggle with the same affliction currently destroying my sanity.

"Fuck—" he wheezes, and in nearly just the same way he had that afternoon with his cock in his hand. I promptly start to sweat.

"You alright, bro?" a voice calls from near the staircase— James' voice, of course, as he comes traipsing back downstairs in fresh shorts.

Luke heads to the sink to cough, but he takes a brief moment once there to flip off the general direction of the stairs.

James laughs, a rich sound that travels over the commotion of the television and the voices of our friends. He crosses the room easily, patting Bryan on the back as he passes, and I step aside so he can access the fridge. "I came here for you, not a drink," he tells me, and he slips an arm around my waist. Still, he opens the fridge as he speaks, and he pulls me in front of him as he rummages inside. "Have I told you lately that you smell incredible?" he asks, and I hear the desire in his voice just as I feel it in his cock tucked into the waistband of his shorts. Against my back, he twitches, which means he'd kept his word. He hasn't come yet either, and he's still eager. *Lord*, is he eager. "Seriously, babe, I don't know if it's your hair or your skin or what, but you—"

His hand presses flat against my stomach, holding me to him, and the heat of it burns my flesh. "Now you're just being cruel."

He laughs against my ear, pulls forth a beer, and shuts the fridge. "A bit, yes, although I think you've been crueler to Luke. I need to go see if he's still alive. Remember, he's no good to either of us dead." With that, he releases me, and he saunters across the kitchen to perch by Luke's side with his shit-eating grin intact.

I take off too, and mostly out of spite. I go to join Annette and Cassie at the table, although it's hard to keep my mind on their conversation when all I can think about is the night before, when James had spread me wide across that very table while Luke had watched from behind a closed door with his cock in his hand. Although arousal never fully leaves my system, it does die down a bit as the night progresses, only to spike in a fever pitch at random times thanks to words or looks from one of the two of the objects of my desire.

"I can't believe you're *not wearing panties*," Luke whispers furiously when we catch a moment together in the living room. "For *fuck's* sake, when James told me you were totally bare under that dress, and so wet you're practically soaking your thighs, I—do you have any idea what that's *doing* to me, Davidson?"

Yet again, my pussy clenches at the use of my last name and the utterly Luke way that he says it. "So close it down," I shoot back, the words barely breathed. "Convince everyone to go to bed and put me out of my misery, because I'm—Jesus, I want you both so bad that I'm *aching*, Luke."

His throat contracts at the word 'both,' but I don't even fumble over it. I'm too far gone, too in deep for them both, for it to even give me pause. Both of them, both of them *together*, is simply just what my body needs.

"So you're ready, are you?" James asks me later still. He wraps an arm around my waist in the dining room, once again drawing my back to his front, and he speaks the words into my ear. "Luke says you're ready for us to take you somewhere nice and quiet and undo all the pretty buttons on your dress." James has taken apart the very buttons that span from the bodice of my dress to the hem enough times that I'm almost more used to the sight of it on my floor than on my body. As if to prove his point, his fingers twist expertly around a button atop my stomach. In a flash, he has the fabric separated. In another, he closes it again. "Ah, Luke saw," he says, brushing a kiss behind my ear. "In the kitchen. He's trying to talk to Grant, but he can't keep his eyes off you. Look. Look at him, babe."

I do, of course. It's hard not to. My eyes flit to Luke on instinct alone, and I spy him staring directly at us with his eyes on fire. My next breath comes in shakily, and James feels it. His muscular forearm flexes beautifully against my waist, and Luke's gaze flickers downwards, taking in the sight, before he turns forcefully away.

James laughs, and his breath tickles my neck. "Poor guy." For a moment, he pauses, his nose nuzzling my skin. What follows comes out quieter still, and more thoughtful, with amusement no longer present in his tone. "I can't imagine what it's like to not be able to touch you whenever I want. I know how it used to feel, anyway, back before we got together, and—man, that shit sucked. I actually feel kind of bad for him."

I lace my fingers through the hand atop my waist. "So put us *both* out of our misery, and you too," I tell him, craning my head back to look at him. He looks back, his lips gently parted and his stubble dark across his jaw. "If anyone can convince people to go to bed, it's you. We're both waiting on that—waiting on *you*."

His eyes flicker between each of mine, keen and searching. "Yeah. I know." He presses a kiss to my forehead. "You're sure you want to do this?"

"Do you?"

"Desperately."

Tension melts from between my shoulder blades, tension I hadn't even felt gather, and I know he feels it. "Good, because—baby, I'm seriously about to start begging you to fuck me right here in front of everyone. Don't make me do that."

He smiles slowly, his fingers squeezing mine atop my stomach. "Oh, that's hot. I could get very into that, but—not tonight. I want this dress off you now."

I never do fully find out how he does it, but, with feigned yawns and absent mentions of his own alleged exhaustion, he somehow has everyone ready for bed within a half hour. It's masterful, really, some one-two punch that he begins and then Luke picks up, and it doesn't surprise me at all to see them succeed. They're unstoppable together, the two of them. They always have been.

"I'm off," Luke says after most everyone else has trudged upstairs. Alongside me and James, only Aaron and Cassie remain, the pair sequestered together in cozy seats upon the sofa. "'Night, guys."

After he opens his door, he throws a look towards where James has me held atop his lap at the table. *You better fucking hurry up,* he says with only his eyes, or maybe that's just the way I want to take it. Yet again, I can't quite tell where his desire begins or where mine ends, but I can feel James' desire pressed firmly against my ass.

After the door closes, James kisses my cheek, and then my jaw, and then my neck. He sweeps my hair aside, trails his lips over my pulse point, and skims his fingers along my knee. "I'll take you in there as soon as they go upstairs," he promises quietly into my skin, and I know he means Aaron and Cassie, but I hardly even realize that they're there. The combination of his lips and his fingers and his voice has me transfixed. "And I want to watch you with him first. I want you to put on a little show for me." His hand covers my thigh and squeezes gently. "I want to see his face when you undo every last one of these buttons. I want you to show him how good you look, and how good you taste, and how good you feel. Will you do that for me, Mills?"

I grip his wrist and nudge his fingers higher, my own voice just as soft. "Yes. Whatever you want, baby."

It works exactly right. He groans into the side of my neck. "Good girl," he says, his fingers swirling higher, and—

"Seriously, you two?" Cassie demands. My eyes snap open to find her staring at us with a unique mixture of amusement and disgust. It's the same way she's looked at us for years. "James, are you seriously about to finger her under the table right now?"

I don't have to look at James to know he grins. I hear it in his voice, which remains tucked in my neck, although he speaks up louder for her to hear. "Sure, if I have to, but I'm really hoping you two will take the hint and get out of here so I can fuck her where you're sitting. It's a personal goal of mine to get her off everywhere in this house. You'd be surprised where all we've—"

They clear out quickly, thank god, although Cassie chucks a pillow our way as she leaves.

"You're an idiot," I tell him, laughing. "Such an idiot, seriously—"

If he listens, he doesn't show it. "Up," he says, his tone suddenly curt. "Off my lap. I've been actively hurting for—I don't even know, the last hour, maybe. I need to come."

"You could have convinced everyone to go to bed much—"

He lifts me himself, sets me on my feet, and tugs me by the hand towards Luke's door. "Sure I could have, but you look so fucking hot when you're all desperate and needy. It was worth waiting and hurting just to watch you squirm."

He doesn't knock. He tosses open the door like he owns it, the same as he does to the door to our room, and Luke's head snaps towards us so quickly that it looks like it hurts. If it does, he doesn't let on. He sits on the edge of his bed, the covers pulled tight and surprisingly neat, with his hand already cupped around himself through his shorts. Just at that—at next to *nothing*, really—my mouth dries with want.

James closes the door behind us carefully; the latch catches with a quiet click. Hand still wrapped around mine, he joins Luke in simply looking at me, and it hits me suddenly.

After all the leadup, all the promise, all the possibility, none of us really know what we're doing.

James kisses me, his lips feather-light and unexpectedly tender. It's the sort of kiss that one might give after the end of a successful first date, although that hadn't held true for us. Years before, when he'd gone to kiss me after walking me to my door, he hadn't held back. Moreover, I hadn't wanted him to. His mouth had transformed from questioning to passionate as soon as he'd felt me meet him halfway—*more* than halfway, maybe, because I'd wanted him so badly by that point that I'd all but dragged him inside. Yet it feels like he asks me another question now, all these years later and all over again, just with the gentle pressure of his mouth ghosting against mine once, twice, a third time. His thumb strokes the back of my knuckles, the motion unexpectedly tender as well, and I press my hand flat to the warmth of his chest, feel his heart race under my palm, and breathe in the question he asks.

"I want to watch," he says again, just as he had in the dining room, but also differently still. I know he means to tell Luke more than me, but he growls the words into my mouth, and they send a shiver down the length of my spine. "Take your dress off for us, babe. Show us how wet you are."

Us. God, that does almost *evil* things to my body, but I love it.

He lets me go, takes purposeful strides towards an

armchair in the corner of the room, and chucks Luke's overflowing bag unceremoniously onto the floor. A couple shirts spill out, loose across the carpet, and he sits down with tension roping across his body. He perches quite literally on the edge of his seat, his arms leaned onto his knees and his hands clasped tightly together, and he just *looks* at me. That's all. He simply looks, his dark hair tumbled into matching eyes and his strong jaw taut and his long fingers clenched, and he steals my breath.

"Are you sure?" Luke asks. The stroke he gives his cock, his golden forearm flexing, guarantees that my lack of breath is here to stay. His eyes, hot like boiling honey, flicker towards James for the briefest of moments before looking back to me. "You can start with her if you want. I don't—"

"No," James says, the answer firm. "You got to watch last night. I *made* you watch last night. It's my turn. Make her come. Show her off for me. She promised me a show."

"*Fuck*," Luke says, fierce and low, and he strokes again. Without taking his eyes off me, or his hand from his cock, he leans and yanks open the top drawer of his nightstand. After a moment of rummaging, he plucks forth a box of condoms. "Ducked out to the store earlier," he explains. "I was hard the entire time just thinking about this. You—"

My fingers find the top button of my dress, and, just like that, his vocal chords give out. Unexpected power courses through me as I slip the button free. "I'm on—" I pause, but then I stop. I look to James, the question unspoken.

James meets my gaze unwaveringly. "When were you last tested?" he asks. "Are you clean?"

It takes Luke another button to realize who James addresses, and then another button to respond. "I—it's been a few months, but I tested clean and haven't been near anyone since. I've been—"

"Too busy jerking it to Millie?"

The way Luke tips his head, a bit of smile present, doesn't exactly disagree. "—in a dry spell, I was going to say, but—"

"Look at her. Tell her the truth. You know she wants to hear it."

My heart pounds in my ears, in my neck, in my chest, and in between my legs, as the fourth, fifth, and sixth buttons open. My breasts spill free, my nipples peaked and red and exposed, and Luke makes a sound that I can almost taste. "For the love of god, Davidson—" he breathes, and he tugs his cock again, harder. A damp spot appears just above the grip of his fist. His eyes rove across my chest and sear into my hands, and with such intensity that I could swear that his gaze, not my fingers, undoes the next button. "You're so fucking beautiful, and you're going to ruin me. You've *already* ruined me. There's no way I'm ever going to want anyone else like this."

It makes next to no sense, but the power boiling in my blood crests, twists with something that feels an awful lot like possessiveness, and might give me pause if I had more control over my own faculties. I feel that sense of deep ownership over James, of course, and have for years, but… Luke? I have absolutely no claim over him, none whatsoever. He isn't *mine*, much as—

Much as I might want him to be. Him and James both.

Fuck.

"I'm on the pill," I tell him, releasing another button, and then another, and then another. My navel peaks out, and Luke stares as if he means to burn the image into his mind. "If you don't want to use a condom—"

James nods his approval, glances towards Luke, and begins to grin. It stretches across his face slowly, lighting up his features, and he leans back in his chair. "You broke his brain, babe."

Indeed, Luke stares, his eyes locked on mine. His mouth

had fallen open at some point, and he closes it after a moment, only to open it again and lick his lips. "Keep going," he demands, and I only realize then that I've stopped the progress of my buttons just as I've reached my hips. "Keep going and—say it."

Somehow, I know what he means. "I'm on the pill," I tell him again, and he swallows. His throat constricts roughly once and then a second time, as if he struggles with even that basic function. "If you want, you can—no, *I* want you to come inside me." The admittance earns a duo of groans, one from each of them, and I can hardly stand it. Desire spikes inside me, hot and thick. "James is the only one I've ever let fuck me bare, but—I trust you. If you want—"

"There's nothing like it," James says. He tugs his cock over the waistband of his shorts, and he fondles the red, swollen head with a lazy palm. When he catches me watching, his smile widens. "Seriously, *nothing* like it. You won't believe how good it feels to come inside her."

"*Fuck*, Davidson—" It bursts from Luke almost savagely, like a culmination of several things that remain unspoken. It sounds that way, at least, as he pulls his own shorts and boxer down and off in one swoop. It leaves him entirely bare, every toned muscle beautifully exposed and held perilously tight, and his hand goes to his cock with a grip that looks almost painful. He's every bit as impressive as James, a little longer but not quite as thick, and my mouth waters at the wet sound of his fist gathering precum from his leaking tip to smear down his length. He groans, growls, thrusts up into his hand, and his eyes squeeze closed for less than a breath before he opens them again. "Take your dress off," he says, a second demand, and he licks his lips again, the swipe of his tongue quick. "Take it off and then get over here and get *on* me already, because—I need to feel you. I need you to drench my fingers, and then—I'm going to lick you until you soak my face. Come on, Davidson. Hurry up and get over here so I can make you come, because I need—"

I slip two of the last several buttons free and uncover my pussy to his eager gaze. He sucks in a deep, harsh breath, words once again cut abruptly short, but James speaks up for him.

"Go on, babe," he says, his voice soft, almost sweet. He slides his grip down his cock, rubs a slow hand across his balls, and then makes a fist to stroke back up. "Be a good girl and listen to Luke."

I snap.

Nothing else explains it entirely. Suddenly, my nerves simply fracture, and it feels as though someone has pushed me off some impossibly high cliff and left me to free fall. It's almost *too* much, the sight of the pair of them with their cocks swollen and rigid and Luke's strokes a furious pace in comparison to the purposeful caresses of James' hand. I've had this same fantasy more times than I can count, of both of them hard and desperate and waiting for me, but it's the first time I've ever actually experienced it, and without a stitch of the guilt that usually colors dreams had both during the day and night. Details flash before my eyes at random—the gleaming brilliance of Luke's golden hair, the tense hold of James' wrists, the strong chords of Luke's calves, the broad stretch of James' shoulders—and they're both so beautiful, and both so very *mine*, that a series of whimpers flea from my mouth as I make quick work of the last of the buttons.

"Finally," Luke says, the word ground out deeply from his chest, as I let the slender straps fall from my shoulders. The entire stretch of black linen crumples into a heap upon the floor. "*Finally*, fuck, come here, come here—"

I go to him, let him yank me to him impatiently, and feel the slickness of his precum spread across one cheek as he grips my ass in both hands and brings me down to straddle his lap.

"*Fuck*," he repeats, weaker than before, as he drags me over the top of his erection. The lips of my pussy part slightly as he pulls, pushes, pulls, pushes, his fingertips digging into my ass while I slide over him, the glide easy from my arousal. My arms reach for him, slide around his neck and grip, and he captures my mouth for a long, bruising kiss full of twisting tongues and panting breaths. "I could—god, I could come just from *this*," he says, and he swallows my whimpers by chasing down my lips again. "How—James, how do you stand it? How hot she sounds? How incredible she looks? How good she feels? It's not—"

"Practice." For the first time, James sounds a little choked up. When I glance over my shoulder to look at him, I find him flushed, his cheeks growing with a heat that matches the swollen tip of his cock. His left hand grips the arm of the chair so hard that his knuckles have gone white, and the casual perusal of his erection has become a thing of the past. He strokes firmly, quickly, his eyes locked where Luke's fingers surely bruise my flesh. "So much practice—*Jesus*—and —" Belatedly, he finds me looking at him, and he groans. "Babe," he says, and it sounds like a plea. "Babe, you look— you look so *fucking* good, riding him like that." It tugs a moan from me, and then Luke elicits another when his hips buck in response to the clenching of my pussy. "I've only ever seen you ride me, and the angle—it's all different. Fuck, the way your ass looks right now—"

Luke's lips close around the tight twist of my neck, and he sucks. "Let me turn you around," he says, and his teeth follow. He bites, licks, and bite again. "Let me spread you wide so James can watch while you get yourself off on my cock. And I'll—"

James swears spectacularly, and Luke dips his mouth

lower, his lips and tongue and teeth teasing as he heads for my breasts. I arch into his face, my head tipping back and back bending with it, and I hear James swear again, louder still. "And touch me," I beg. "Please touch me. *Please.*"

"Everywhere," Luke promises darkly as his tongue twists across my nipple. When I whine, he takes it into his mouth and sucks. "I'm going to touch you *everywhere*, Davidson, so you—*fuck*, I forgot that you—if me calling you that makes you tighten that much when you're barely touching me, I don't even—I'm going to last ten seconds inside you. That's all there is to it."

"I'm going to rub one out before I fuck her mouth," James says. "I've been hard for way too long, and I want to enjoy her. The things she can do with her tongue—just fucking wait. She's—oh, god, Mills, *look* at you—" He almost moans the latter, the words passed difficultly through what sounds like a swiftly-closing throat, and all because Luke follows through with his promise and turns me to face him.

Luke moves me easily, like my body is the most pliable of clays to toss and turn between powerful hands. He brings my back flush to his chest and spreads my legs wide, positioning them on either side of his thighs. Immediately, his mouth picks up the work he'd abandoned on my chest. He drags his tongue across the vein that throbs in my neck, and his fingers slide upwards, crawling up overheated skin. Soon, he reaches slickness as his fingertips swirl up my inner thighs and slowly approach my aching pussy. "No, none of that," he says when my head falls back against his shoulder. "Look at James. You promised him a show, he said, and you know he wants to see your face."

"I do," James says, and tighter still. "I really, really do. Look at me, Davidson."

As always, hearing my last name sets my insides on fire. I gasp, squirm across Luke's lap, and then lift my legs to bend at the knee until my shins press to the mattress on either side of his thighs. It allows me to move across Luke's cock just as before, and Luke gives a groan into my neck that I feel reverberate throughout every cell in my body.

"I can't believe—" Luke sucks in a breath. "I can't believe you've been calling her *my* nickname for her, you dick," he says as his fingers twist slowly higher. "How long have you been getting her off on—oh, holy shit. Holy *shit*." His fingers freeze, gripping almost painfully, and then vanish from my thighs altogether. Once again, he grabs my ass, but with a slower caress than before. His fingertips trail, dragging upwards across my cheeks, and then he gives a brief, experimental squeeze. "Your ass is *unreal*, babe. It's—for fuck's sake, there aren't *words—*"

If James spies the hypocrisy in Luke stealing *his* nickname for me, he doesn't call him on it. I don't either, but my body certainly catches it, even if my brain doesn't. My pussy clenches again in another desperate spasm, and I lean forward a little, placing my hands on his knees, as he strokes a smooth path where my cheeks meet my thighs. "Luke," I say, my voice breathless. "I want you to touch me. You promised. You said—"

"I will," he says quickly, and he rocks me against his cock once, twice, a third time, the pace increasing in fervor. "I will, I swear. Just—yeah, lean forward more. Let me look at you. Yeah, just like that. *Just* like that. Oh, that's it. That's—"

James seals it all. "Good girl, Mills," he says, his eyes boring into mine. "She's *such* a good girl, isn't she, Luke?"

When I moan, Luke grunts, the sound harsh, almost animalistic. He picks up the thread immediately. "The *best*," he says, and I feel him shift behind me, his chest suddenly absent from my back as if he's leaned away. "The very best. Davidson, show me how good you can be. Touch yourself for me. I want to feel you come on my cock, just like this, while

James and I watch. Give me a preview of—*fuck*—of how good it's going to feel later when I'm inside you."

I'm helpless to resist, and I wouldn't want to resist even if I could. When I dip my fingers in between my thighs, reaching for the bundle of nerves that has ached for hours, I nearly come with a single rub.

"Good girl," James says again, and my hips jerk erratically as my pussy grinds on Luke's cock. James' eyes dance, flicking repeatedly from my hand between my thighs, to my swaying breasts, to my face, to whatever Luke does behind me. My eyes, on the other hand, never leave his face. "You should see him," he says, his brow furrowing. He bites his lip briefly, and I know, then, that his end is near too.

The first end, at least. I can't wait for the second, and the third, and the fourth—

"Look at him, Mills," he presses. "How many times, bro? How many times have you imagined watching her ass move like that while she rides your cock?"

I turn my head to find Luke leaned back on one forearm, his golden eyes locked on my ass and one hand tracing light, almost ticklish patterns across my left cheek. "Too many to count," he says. "Although I'm inside her in those fantasies, but—this is already so good it doesn't even compare. *God*, it doesn't compare." Only after he speaks does he realize that I watch him. The second our eyes meet, he groans. "*Fuck*," he hisses through his teeth. "Fuck, Davidson, you—" His arm on the mattress tenses, and he grips the comforter in between his fingers. "I'm going to come, and then I'm going to eat you out until I'm hard enough to fuck you just like we talked about." On my ass, his hand contracts too, and my toes curl against my feet. "Just like this, but on your knees. On your knees, so James can fuck your mouth, that perfect mouth that —*fuck*—that sucked my cum off your fingers after I came on your tits this afternoon—"

"*Fuck.*" James comes at that, and I turn just in time to see him close one hand over the head of his cock to catch the mess that erupts. It drips from his palm, spilling onto the floor, as he strokes himself through it with an aggressive hand. That, combined with the look on his face and the heat in his voice, undoes me. "Yes—god, Mills, *yes—*" he says, the final affirmation nearly sworn, as I pulse faster and faster underneath my fingers and then tip over the edge entirely. "So beautiful—you're *so* beautiful—"

Luke must drop back fully, because suddenly both his hands close over my hips to rock me through the spasms that pull all of the muscles in my body tight, unbearably tight, and then release in a flood. I cry out with it, a sharp, frantic noise I don't even try to stifle, and then—

Luke comes too, spilling heavily against his leg and the comforter and a little onto my leg as well. "Yes—yes—*fuck* yes—" he says, panting, as his cock jerks underneath me. His cum smears back across his cock, dragged there by my pussy, and he groans. "Oh, you're—you're *so* fucking good, Davidson, *Jesus—*"

My hair is in my mouth by the time I come back down to earth, drawn there by breaths sucked deep. When I lift a shaking hand to pull it free, I taste myself on my fingers, and James' soft sigh of satisfaction opens eyes I hadn't realized I'd closed.

"Lick them for me," he instructs. Carelessly, he wipes the mess in his hand down one leg of the shorts he still hasn't taken off. His other hand still tugs at his cock, but slower, far slower, and his eyes have gone soft rather than crackling with rampant electricity. He gives a quiet, gentle hum as I take the tips of my fingers into my mouth to suck lightly. "You know how much I love that. What'd Luke do this afternoon when you licked his cum clean from your fingers?"

Just to make him groan, I take my fingers deeper, and my

stomach flutters when he does. "He finished absolutely covering me," I tell him, sliding my fingers free to ghost across my lips, and James laughs breathlessly.

Behind me, Luke laughs identically. "Your fault, Davidson," he says. Slowly, his fingers release my hips, and the caresses that follow paint a gentle path up my lower back before sliding down again to trace across the backs of my thighs. Each stroke feels like a silent compliment. "It was the hottest thing that had ever happened to me—at least then. This tops it, but I think everything with you must just get better all the time."

"It does," James assures him. Casually, with his long body stretching, he finally drops the last of his clothes and kicks his shorts and underwear aside. "See, I knew you'd get it. I knew you'd appreciate her and worship her like I do. I just *knew*. No one else—"

Luke's hands still. He waits. Atop him, I do too.

"That's it," James says after a moment. "Just—no one else." It sounds like an instruction, as is what follows. "Eat her out. I want to see her face while you do it. She's usually squirming so much that I can't get a good enough look at her, and—I could stare for hours at all the faces she makes." He smirks a little. "Unless you're too tired. Did she wear you out?"

No one else.

It promises something deeply coveted, something I've already started to hope for but haven't yet assumed: this might not be a one-time thing.

Luke gives a snort of laughter. "No. I'll sleep when I'm dead—maybe literally. It's like I told her earlier: I don't fully expect to survive her. Still, I'm going to die happy." He's still chuckling as he moves me with the same commanding ease as before, and he guides my body off of his like he's spent multiple years positioning me in any way he'd like instead of just dreaming about it. Quickly, he has me stretched out on my back, and he bends to snag his discarded boxers with one hand. With such care it catches my breath, he gently wipes his cum from where it dries on my thighs, and then cleans his legs and half-hard cock as well. Last, he makes some attempt to dab at the comforter, although it looks perfunctory at best. He's far too eager to drop his boxers and join me again on the bed, a truth I see all over the eyes that never leave my body.

"James?" I ask just as that happens. Luke stills halfway atop me, but he resumes his movements when I widen my legs further to make room for his body. I turn to find James also at half-mast, his fingers stroking almost absently along his balls. "Would you have—" The question dies partway on my lips as Luke kisses my neck so softly that I might as well melt into the bed. I sigh, wind a hand into his hair, and sigh again when he dips a kiss a millimeter lower. "Would you have let us do this sooner if Luke and I had both told you that we wanted it?"

Interest halts the path of Luke's lips. He waits, listening, his weight solid and his body entirely relaxed against mine. It makes for an incredible change of pace from the normal all-encompassing tightness of his muscles that seem to seize whenever I'm around, a fact I've always noted, even if I hadn't wanted to assume its meaning.

I can see James consider my question. I watch the wheels turn in his head, watch his mouth pull thoughtfully to one side, watch him cup his balls and just barely squeeze. "Not at first," he says finally. "I wanted you all to myself for a while. There was no way I—"

"For a while?" Luke repeats into my neck. Even as he nips at my skin, he still makes the question sound skeptical. "You'd still like to kill any guy who even flirts with her, let alone—"

"Not you."

Luke's fingers dance down the sides of my body, moving in tandem with one another and lifting goosebumps on my skin. "Why?"

"I told you—I knew you'd get it. I knew you'd worship her just like I do. And, besides—" For a moment, James pauses, his lips parted and his eyes thoughtful. "You're my two favorite people, and I know you both feel that way about me and each other too. This—the three of us—it just…makes sense."

It does. God, it does, and not just because his eyes could surely convince me of anything at this moment, just like Luke's tongue twisting against my collarbone could do the same.

"Now, go on," James says. It doesn't sound like a suggestion.

Luke follows through, although slowly. He drags each moment out with slow patterns of his lips, and gentle sweeps of his tongue, and careful strokes of his fingers, all as he covers every inch of skin from my neck to my knees—or it feels that way, at least. He seems intent on tasting and caressing and kissing every part of me at least once, and each move acts like a careful experiment intended to draw forth a reaction that he files away in a far corner of his brain for later use. "There?" he demands, his voice gruff, as my back arches uncontrollably at a soft flick of his tongue against the sensitive skin where my breast meets my ribs. "Like that?" he asks, lower still, when he twists his fingers in excruciating repetitions atop my hipbones and my hips buck forward unbidden. "Is this what you want?" he teases as he sucks lightly along my inner thighs, his breath tickling and his nose nuzzling and his tongue tracing as he inches closer and closer to my pussy.

I spread my legs wider, my breath a shaky pant and my body aching once again. *"No,"* I tell him, the word broken, as I tug his hair with impatient fingers. "Luke, you—you *know* what I want."

"Tell me," he prompts. He bites gently at the crease where my leg meets my pelvis, and my hips jump again. Sucking in a deep breath, he groans. "God, you smell good," he says, and his tongue dips out to lick the spot he's just bitten. He groans again, louder. "And you taste—fuck, it's all over your thighs, and it's—I'm going to get addicted to this. There's no way around it." He licks again, his tongue ghosting the outside of my folds, and then he swears a second time. "Fuck, James, you should see how wet she is."

I wrench my eyes open, and fresh heat breaks across my body when I see James. He's leaned forward in his seat, his hand still around his cock, which has grown stiff again in his palm. When he sees me watching him, his cock twitches noticeably in his grip. "Can I?" he asks, already halfway on his feet.

The eagerness in his voice clenches my muscles anew, and Luke huffs a laugh into my pelvis. "You have to now," he says, pressing kisses gently all around my opening. "She's gushing just thinking about it."

James joins us quickly, and the bed creaks softly under his weight as he sits next to me. I immediately take one hand from Luke's hair to reach for his cock, but he bats me away. "None of that," he says, and then he gathers both my wrists and pins them above my head with one strong hand. "I want your mouth, not your—"

"Oh, she *loves* that," Luke says, his teeth zeroing into another spot on my thigh. He latches on for a moment that passes all too briefly, and then he pulls back and sits up, stretching his neck as he does. "Look at her, man." He sounds proud of himself, and his face shines with it too, as well as with a wet smear down his chin. My body twitches in response, my clit throbs, my pussy pulses, and it all increases tenfold when he reaches down to give his cock a brief squeeze. "Look at how fucking *gone* she is."

My brain disappears further still when James uses his free hand to stroke my breast. His fingertips ghost across one peaked nipple, pinch gently, and then he roughly palms my breast in a complete juxtaposition to his prior caresses. Quickly, I'm rendered into a mess of even louder whimpers and pleas, those that only increase when Luke skims his own hands up my thighs. "Please," I beg, lifting my hips, arching my back, opening my legs as far as they'll go. Luke squeezes his cock again at the latter. "Please just—touch me, lick me, *something*. I can't stand it, having both of you this close but not—"

James trails a callused finger down my quivering stomach. "Are you going to come for Luke?"

Luke's hips jerk upwards into his fist, and I can only cry out as James' finger stops mere inches away from my clit. "Yes," I promise. "Yes, or you, or—or *both*, but please—" He offers me a reward at that, perhaps specifically at the use of the word 'both,' because that's when he releases a rumble from his chest.

He slides a smooth circle atop my clit, a motion he's made so many times over the years that it surely numbers in the millions, and then swipes his fingers down to sink into me. He curls them with a flex of his wrist, tearing a cry from my throat, and then draws them back out to lick. "So good," he says, his tongue twisting around his fingers, and it doesn't even sound like a taunt, although my aching pussy takes it as one. It sounds genuine, just as it always has, and he sucks his fingers brutally, harshly, with a deep, primal sound. "Make her come," he says, the words addressed to Luke, who stares at him a hazy expression of his own, and—

Luke does, as simply as that.

He all but dives back between my thighs, his tongue flat

and hot and insistent as he paints one broad lick along the lips of my pussy, and then another, and then another. His moan twists up my body, and, in turn, I twist my wrists against James' hand to no avail. At that, Luke cups his hands underneath my ass and tilts my hips upwards. His tongue slides inside me, swirling, furious, almost punishing, and a sob wracks my body in aching relief.

"I told him how much you love that," James says from somewhere near my side, and I hear him, but I also don't. All the attention I have is located below my waist, where Luke seems determined to lick every last drop of wetness from me. Still, I can hear the thickness of James' tone and the arousal it imparts, and it brings even further joy to the relief flooding my system. He returns his fingers to my breast, where they slide, still wet from my arousal and his mouth, and he pinches roughly at my nipple. "More times than I can count, I've told him how good you taste and how wet you get and how much you love my tongue. How's he doing, babe? Is he giving you what you want?"

He waits for an answer, something he makes even clearer when he pinches my nipple again. The pleasurable pain brings me back to myself a little even as Luke tilts me higher, until my hips are more off the mattress than on. "Yes," I say, and I feel Luke's hips rebound off the mattress. "But—also no. I want his fingers too, and I want—my clit. That's what I need to come. I—"

"Tell him that."

So I do, even as I feel Luke's fingertips brush my opening underneath his jaw as if he waits right alongside James. "Use your fingers," I tell him, and his hips thrust again. Somewhere above me, James gives a familiar, throaty laugh. "And lick my clit. Suck it. Suck it, *please*, and I'll—"

Luke growls into my pussy, and his fingers strike, sliding inside me in one smooth motion. He growls again, and his tongue slides up, swirling against my clit in the same motion that James had rubbed. "Holy shit," Luke says, the words hot, burning me, branding me, making me sweat. "Holy *shit*, you're tight, Davidson—"

I clench around his fingers, and then clench a second time when James commands, "Curl your fingers. Curl them, and you'll feel it. You'll feel it when you—*there.*"

It's an unnecessary announcement, but one that sounds outside of his control. In turn, I can't control the cry that leaves my lips as Luke brushes against gold inside me. I buck into his mouth with abandon as he lavishes attention on my clit, his tongue twisting and twirling and his lips sucking, sucking beautifully, as sparks shoot across my body. "Oh— oh, *god*," I whimper, I whine, I moan, a repetition of agonized, pleased, endless pleas that carry on for what feels like ages. "Oh, please—*fuck*, that's—Jesus Christ, Luke, you feel—I'm so *close*—"

James' hand slides up my chest, caresses my neck, strokes my cheek. "Look at Luke, Mills," he says eventually, yet another command, but one given more softly than most. I open my eyes to find him staring hungrily at my face as his chest rises erratically with his breath. He's gloriously flushed, his cheeks as red as the tip of his cock, and his head falls back briefly as he strokes his length. "Look at how much he's enjoying your pussy. Look at how bad he wants you. *Look* at him."

I do, and I spy Luke's golden eyes staring up between my thighs, his mouth moving tirelessly atop my clit, his body continuing to flex into the mattress with each fresh sound of pleasure that he drags from my chest. Longing builds, tensing my stomach and promising something even more incredible than the last orgasm he'd given me.

"Your *face*," James says, and his voice chokes a little over the words. He tugs my lower lip free from my teeth and drags his thumb there, the caress slow and sweet. "I could—fuck, I could get used to watching you like this."

That—along with a suck of Luke's lips around my clit, one even harder and more purposeful than all the rest—sends me.

I cry out, my eyes closing, my wrists thrashing, my hips thrusting, my pussy clenching, and with such a cry so harsh that my throat hurts from it afterwards. After a moment, Luke's arm comes to rest across my lower stomach, and he pins me to the mattress to lick me through the pleasure that washes over me in a wave less intense, but still so sweet, that my muscles shatter.

"Keep going," James instructs when Luke's mouth leaves me for a fraction of a second. Instantly, Luke complies, stroking another hot path against me, and then another, and then another. James releases my wrists, and then I feel his head dip as his lips brush across the overheated swell of my throat. "She'll tell you when she's done."

"God," I whisper. It's almost too much, his mouth on my neck and Luke's between my thighs, but I also want more of each. I reach for Luke's hair, feel his head bob against me, and then bury my fingers in the shorter, darker strands of James' hair as well. "God, that was—it's *still—*"

Luke laughs against me, vibrating my clit, as my pussy continues to squeeze his fingers mercilessly. "I told her I finally get why you have such an ego, bro," he says, his lips brushing against me and his arm still holding me down. "The way she carries on—it's enough to give anyone a big head. I've never seen anything like it."

"It's addicting," James says into my neck, and with new fervor in his tone. "Millie, babe—I need you. I need your mouth, and if I need that as badly as I do, I can't imagine how much Luke's hurting."

Luke laughs again, although it's mixed with something of

a swear. "She loves that. She's fucking *obliterating* my fingers, I swear—"

I do love it, love the heavy longing in James' words, and the tender attention of his mouth, and Luke's own resounding need pulsing in his voice. Exhausted muscles or not, power courses through me, and it mixes with desire of my own.

God, they've both been so good to me. I want to make them feel just as good—but I also want them to wait for it, just like they'd made me wait.

Luke laps again at my clit, and I twist as the oversensitive nub pulses. "Okay," I tell him, and he gets the message immediately. He pulls back both his mouth and fingers, and I sit up in time to spy the glistening wetness now across his chin and each of his cheeks. When he catches me looking at him, he licks his lips slowly, savoring the taste, and then wipes his face across one muscular shoulder. "God, Luke, you're a mess—"

"*You're* a mess," he shoots back, his grin instant and broad, and then he drags a hand down his face for good measure. Afterwards, he kisses me, almost as if to prove his point. His lips are impossibly heated, warmed from all the friction he'd built between my legs, and I taste myself on his tongue as it slides across the seam of my lips. He sighs into the kiss, makes a deeper sound when I open my mouth to him, and he crushes my hair into his hand for a brief moment before he lets me go. "Get your ass in the air, Davidson."

James swears as he all but scrambles off the bed, and desire floods my mouth.

They position me themselves, orchestrating my body in a tag-team effort that reminds me of the way they'd convinced everyone to head off for bed. "Come to the edge of the bed, babe, so I can stand—" "Up on your hands and knees, Davidson, there you go—" "Look up at me—fuck, that's it—" "Arch your back—oh, *just* like that, Jesus—" I go along with it, my body warmed with every groan, every swear, every slip of praise, every broken plea. Soon, my fingers are curled around the edge of the mattress, and James stands in front of me, his cock heavy in his hand while Luke positions himself behind me, his hands already gripping my ass.

"Not yet," I warn when I feel Luke line himself up with my entrance, feel him nudge forward the tiniest bit, feel the head of his cock begin to stretch me deliciously as he releases a strangled sound. "I'm still—I'm too sensitive—"

Luke pulls back a fraction of an inch, and then his length presses flush along my opening as his hips flex against my ass. "That's not *helping*, hearing that," he says, the words a growl, and then he slides against me slowly, through the folds of my pussy but not inside me. His lips press against my spine, and his breath trembles. "I *know* how sensitive you are right now—I just felt it with my fingers, for fuck's sake. I know how good it would feel, and I'm about to *lose* it, seriously—"

James winds a hand into my hair, his muscles tensing as he draws my face forward. "Good girl," he says lowly as I drag my tongue along the crease of his hip, and his fingers squeeze my scalp gently. He smells like him, of the crisp pine of his skin and the familiar musk of his cum, and he strokes his cock beside my face as I lick the scent from his thighs. "God, Mills, you're—take me in your mouth, babe. Come on. I've been dreaming about it all—"

"Not yet," I say, and he instantly releases his grip around his cock so I can wrap my fingers around him. He slides smoothly in my hand, slick and wet and deliciously soft and hard at the same time, and my mouth all but waters. "Soon, but—not until I can take Luke. It's not fair otherwise."

As Luke nips at my spine, which arches my back further, James exhales a laugh. "Is that the game you're playing?" he asks, and his free hand comes to rest underneath my chin so that his fingers can stroke my throat. When I suck beside the base of his cock, my thumb toying with the thick vein that spans the underside of his length, his fingers close gently and I swallow. *"Fuck,"* he grunts, his hips jerking, and I slide my tongue lower, towards his balls. "So—when you swallow me down your pretty throat—" again, his fingers squeeze for just a moment, and I swallow again, "—Luke will know you want him to fuck you? Is that it?"

I glance up at him, paint a slow lick between his testicles, and watch his head fall back helplessly. "Yes."

His head stays there; the muscles of his neck bulge. "Cruel," he rasps. "*So* cruel, and—do that again, babe, but suck this time. Yeah, fuck, like that—like *that*, shit—"

Luke's voice bursts out from behind me, harsh and savage. *"Fuck,"* he repeats, echoing James entirely, and he rocks against me, the grind of his hips hard, almost frantic. "Davidson, that's—*please*—"

They both feel the way that it affects me, James with my breath catching against his skin, Luke with my pussy clenching atop his length. I don't know who moans loudest, me included. "You made *me* wait," I point out, and I lean back, pushing into Luke so I can clear enough space to drag the head of James' cock against my lips. "And James was so patient," I add as James head rocks forward. He's already bitten his lips a fierce, brilliant red, and he stares, fascinated, at the rub of his cock against my mouth. "*So* patient, although he's not getting exactly what he wants right now either."

Luke squeezes my ass reflexively, and his body molds to mine. Quickly, he reaches underneath me, his fingers cupping my breasts, and he squeezes there too. "It's still—fuck, *look* at him, Davidson," he hisses into my ear, and I shiver, flick my tongue out from between my teeth, and catch a drop of James' precum with my tongue. Both of them groan, although I hear Luke's louder as his breath pants hot in my ear. "He's fucking *loving* what you're giving him, and I'm—I want *inside* you already. Show me how far you can take him in your throat so he can feel you moan all around him while I pound you."

James releases my neck, sweeps my hair entirely between both hands, and pulls it back from my face. He holds it there, his forearms flexing, as I twist my tongue slowly around the swollen head of his cock. "God," he says softly, and it sounds like a plea and a prayer both. "God, just—again, babe. And, Luke—" He sucks in a deep breath, his brow furrowing as I listen and slide my tongue slower, gathering the taste of him, savoring every sight and sound he offers just as I savor Luke's rough caresses on my breasts. "Convince her. Touch her. Tease her. Her clit is right there. Fucking *use* it."

Luke drops his hands lower, shifts my thighs apart with flexing fingers, and dips a finger between my soaking folds. "Killing me," he says, his lips skimming the freshly-exposed back of my neck, and he sucks the sweat that gathers at my hairline. "You're *killing* me, you know that?" He slides a smooth finger over my opening, his hips rocking at the same time, and he drags the pads of his fingertips to my clit. It throbs under his fingers, sensitive and pulsing but no longer uncomfortable, and he rubs slowly, smoothly, with a gentle nudge back and forth. "I want to make this good for you, Davidson, but—there's going to come a time when I lose control and just *use* you. It's taking everything in me not to tear you away from James right now, shove your gorgeous face into the mattress, and fuck you until you squeeze my cock like I had you squeezing my fingers."

Heat rises in my cheeks, and I pause the slow path of my lips up James' length, freezing a kiss held part-way down his shaft.

James tugs gently at the back of my head, and I look up at

him to find him staring back, his eyes more dark and open and full of lust than I've ever seen. "Oh, she likes that," he says, and I lick my way down the rest of him. When I reach his balls, he holds me there, and I suck eagerly as he shoves desperately against my tongue. "Can you—*fuck*—" He gives a series of shaking breaths as I let my mouth roam as far as he'll allow me to go. "Can you feel it, Luke? Can you feel how she's—"

"*Yes.*" It sounds like relief as Luke rears back, away from me, and spreads my legs wider for inspection. "And I can see it." He slides his fingers inside me, and I moan into James' skin, a moan that makes him clutch me tighter and makes Luke spread me wider still. "She's so wet and ready, and she's —Davidson, what do you want? What's it going to take for you to let me have you? Whatever it is—whatever you want —it's yours. But I'm—"

I can't answer because James' hands won't let me, but I'm also too focused on the sound of Luke's words—and the way James moans with each exhale—to speak.

James answers for me, and correctly, too. "Keep going," he urges, and, at first, I think he means me. "Keep going," he says again, dissuading me of the notion, and I wonder if he and Luke make eye contact across my bent head and arched back. The thought makes my legs tremble. "Beg her. That's what she wants. And—line your cock up with her to nudge her like you were before. It'll be torture for you, but she loves it. She probably loves it *because* it's torture, and—god, I love you, Mills. I love your mouth and I love your devious little mind and I love your perfect body and I love how fucking wet you are for me and for Luke and for—*fuck*—for *both* of us—"

Luke slides his fingers from me, and when I pull back, leaning my hips to search for Luke behind me, James lets me go in part. His hands remain in my hair, but he gives me enough slack to try to catch my breath against his length. "Oh," I breathe when Luke follows James' instruction for the letter. Again, he presses up against my entrance, and he slides wetly, eliciting a moan from us both. "Oh—*oh*—"

Luke rocks into me the tiniest bit, retreats, does the same again, and again, and again. His hands return to my ass, stroking, squeezing, sliding, and the noises that tear at his throat form a true constant. "Please, Davidson—" he says over and over, and it sends the muscles of my thighs closing, clenching together, desperate for friction. "*Shit*," he hisses, and then he shifts his hands downwards, places them on either side of my hips, and grips me tightly. "Shit, you're going to be tight for me, aren't you? And I can't believe you're going to let me come inside you. No one else has but James, you said, and—oh, good girl. *Good girl—*"

My thighs flex as I run my tongue along James' length, swirl my mouth across his tip, lick his cock again. Clearly, Luke understands that this means he's getting somewhere, and James does too.

"Good girl," he repeats, his hips tight from restraint, his voice breaking in his throat, and, *god,* it's almost too much to hear it from both of them. "That's it, babe. Now open your mouth for me. Open your mouth and—"

Luke nudges inside me another inch, and he growls before pulling back. "*Please,*" he repeats again, and more desperate than before. "*Please,* and—I want you to take James in and hold him there, because I'm going to *slam* into you. I want him to feel all the sounds you muffle on his cock, because I know how tight it's going to make your throat. He'll do that for me later, right, James? We'll switch and I'll watch him stretch your tight little pussy and I'll get my turn at your mouth."

"*Yes,*" James says, although if he means to agree to Luke's words or the continued attention of my tongue, I can't tell.

Both, maybe—or probably, based on the way he says it. "Whatever she wants. *Whatever* she wants. It's—"

He doesn't finish, but it doesn't matter. He's already said what I've unknowingly waited for one of them to say all along.

In one smooth motion, I take James deep in my mouth, pull back again to swirl my tongue across his head, and then drag him deeper still. My throat protests the latter, aching as I suck him hard and refuse to let up, but I don't care. I can't care about anything more than the wordless shout of pleasure he gives as his eyes squeeze shut with what looks like overpowering relief. When Luke thrusts into me forcefully, slamming our bodies to meet as promised, any remaining part of my consciousness flees. His thickness stretches me sublimely, his length fills me entirely, his hard hips smack against the underside of my ass, and all with such force that I might literally choke myself on James' cock if both of them hadn't reached out to steady me. As it stands, I still whimper around James' shaft, my throat squeezing in protest as he tickles my gag reflex, but I don't care. I moan against the sensation, a moan that spikes into a higher pitch as Luke pulls out of me slowly, his own moan loud, and then thrusts back in a second time.

"*Millie—*" he says, a rare use of my first name, and in a tone unlike any I've heard him use before. He sounds weak, almost winded, but also nearly angry as he rocks against me. "Millie, you feel—*fuck*, you feel—"

He never does tell me how I feel, but I also don't need to know. His tone says it all, and I feel the exact same way.

"Move for me, babe," James says from somewhere up above me, and, belatedly, I do. I draw him back out so I can suck in a deep breath, and then I take him in again, roll my tongue along the underside of his cock like I know he likes best, and wrap my hand around the base of his cock that I can't yet take inside my mouth. I have to work up to it, and I do, bobbing him deeper with each pass. "Good girl, good girl, good girl—*fuck*, you're so good to me, babe—"

It should have lost its effectiveness by then, the phrase repeated so often and so harshly under his breath, but it hasn't. Each tiny bit of praise clenches my pussy ruthlessly, and Luke grips my hips harder in what feels like both punishment and praise.

"So good—" Luke repeats, picking up the chant, and he slides a hand up my back to clutch my shoulder and steady me further. *"So* good, Davidson, and—squeeze again for me. Squeeze and—"

"Lean," James instructs, and, for a moment, I think he means me. Yet his eyes flit from my face, staring at Luke, and I feel his cock throb in my mouth. "Lean yourself up, because —normally I just shove her down, head to the mattress like you said, because it's the easiest angle to get her to come—"

"I *know*," Luke says, and he sounds like frustration personified. "You've told me—how many fucking times have you told me—"

James ignores him. "Do it after I come," he says, and his eyes briefly slam shut when I release his cock from my hand to draw his entire length further and further into my throat. *"Fuck,* Mills—" he moans, and then his eyes snap open. His gaze paints a hot path across my face, one I feel all the way down in my belly, as he speaks again. "But lean up for now, up so you're more above her and you're going down into her, and then kind of—rock. That'll get her."

Luke listens. He shifts behind me, the muscles of the front of his thighs flexing beautifully against the backs of mine, and then he pushes down with new purpose. It takes several attempts, heated thrusts that smack against my skin, as he searches, and he swears repeatedly under his breath the whole time.

"Look," James demands suddenly, and I know why. I've fit the entire length of him down my throat, until my nose brushes at the patch of hair above his cock that he keeps trimmed close to the skin. "Jesus, Luke, *look* at her."

He's sounded similarly awed before, and truly every time that I've managed to take him that deep—or every time I've gotten near his cock at all, perhaps, because he's nothing if not an eager, verbal partner who lavishes praise. Yet a new note mingles with his awe, a brilliant spike of pride that shines from the dark depths of his eyes, as if it arouses him to no end to show off my skills to someone else.

It arouses me too. *Lord*, does it ever.

"*Shit—*" Luke breathes, and his hips stutter as his cock throbs inside me. "Shit, Davidson, what a fucking *dream* you are—"

Correction: it arouses James to no end to show me off to *Luke*, someone who clearly appreciates me just as much as he does, and it fractures James' carefully-kept patience.

"*Fuck.*" It tears from his throat in a growl, one I know well, and I pull him halfway from my mouth and then suck him deep again, my tongue swirling, to hold him there until my eyes water. "*Fuck,* babe, that's—can I fuck your mouth? Please? I'm—watching you suck me, watching him fuck you —I'm close. Can I—"

I fondle his balls, roll them gently across my palm, and then reach to stroke just behind them. A smooth bundle of nerves awaits, and James fairly shouts when I make contact with what I hope is my clear assent. After the years we've had together, he should know me that well.

He does. He grips my head between his hands to tightly clutch the hair on either side of my ears, and he thrusts eagerly into my mouth. A filthy stream of curses fly from his lips as he holds me in place, the treatment of my mouth rough, frantic, and so erotic that I crave harder thrusts, a tighter hold, more passion. To see him broken so utterly from his typical patience makes me hotter than almost anything else.

Just as he begins to throb in real earnest against my tongue, Luke finds it: the right angle, and the right motion, and the right pressure—and all of it *together*, most difficult of all—to turn the delicious friction between my thighs into something stronger, fiercer, and altogether brighter.

He feels the shift immediately. *"There—"* he groans, the word triumphant. *"There,* Davidson—*there,* right there, *fuck—"*

James grunts when my muffled moans reach a constant around his cock; soon, his own sounds echo, each deeper than the last. *"Yes,"* he says, and I don't know which one of us he eggs on. All three, maybe. "That's it, and—rub her clit, Luke. She'll get so tight you'll—"

"She's *already* tight, so tight I can hardly take it." But Luke listens anyway, and he slips a hand between my clenched thighs. With his own faculties clearly just about shot, it takes him a moment to find my clit, but my entire body seizes when he does. Both men feel it, and both men groan. "Good girl," Luke says, his lips falling to press into my back, and I nearly come just at that. "God, I can't get over how much she *loves* that—"

James' fingers curl against my scalp. "Babe, I'm going to come," he says, the words passed between frantic lips. "And then Luke can bend you the rest of the way over so he can finish you off." He swipes his thumb near my temple, perhaps catching a drip of sweat, and then he moans. His head drops back. "That's it—that's it—*shit*, Millie, *fuck—"*

He spills down my throat, and so far back that I don't even taste him. Still, I suck greedily, eager for every bit he wants to give me, and he pulses repeatedly across my tongue, through my mouth, down my throat, his strangled shout euphoric.

He pulls free far sooner than he normally would, before the last of his aftershocks have gone away, and he pushes my head down as I gasp for breath. "She's fine," I hear him tell Luke when Luke's thrusts falter. "Ask her. Ask her if—"

"Fuck, Luke, *harder*," I beg before he can ask, the words barely above a gasp, but it doesn't matter. Luke hears and he obeys, and my fingers grip the edge of the mattress so tightly that I fear they might crack. "Oh—oh—*oh—*"

James' hand comes to rest on the back of my neck; he traces a faint, soothing pattern across skin made slippery with sweat. "That's it, Mills," he says beside my ear, and I turn my face away from the mattress to find him knelt beside the bed. "Let go, babe," he continues, pressing a kiss into my flushed cheek, my overheated temple, just in front of the curve of my ear. "Let go and come, because Luke won't last much longer, not with how tight this makes you and how good you look and how many times he's imagined fucking you just like this."

I hover on the brink of it, and Luke must too. I can hear him behind me, my name a constant refrain upon his lips, a grunt of, "*Davidson*," spoken with every thrust. His free hand slides up the curve of my spine, palms my ass, and grips me there with an almost painful intensity.

James carries on, his tone unhurried. "I was selfish in wanting your mouth and not your pussy," he continues, and he gathers my hair in his hand, pulls it gently from the back of my neck, and tugs gentler still. I clench around the furious strokes of Luke's cock, gripping him tighter still, and hear Luke add a series of several *fucks* into the repetitious chain of my name. "I mean, I wanted Luke to enjoy fucking you— there really is nothing like it—but I also didn't want to be responsible for making you come. I didn't know if I could hold myself back for long enough to get you there, but I knew he'd work his hardest to make that happen. I just got to enjoy you and watch you enjoy him and watch him enjoy you, and—poor Luke, he's been back there shutting his eyes on and off basically from before he even got inside you. It must be too much for him, and I don't blame him. You're so fucking *hot*, Davidson—"

"Damn it, James, *stop it*," Luke snarls from behind me. "Either help me or shut up, because you're just—you're only making her tighter, and it's making it harder for me not to—"

James' hand slips underneath me, and I feel it slide across my belly, down towards my pulsing clit. "Tell her to come," he says, and I almost feel the moment Luke understands. He inhales sharply, and then he rears back, both hands on my ass, to allow James to take over his work on my clit. "Tell her to come, and—don't say his name, babe. Say mine until you're there, because he's done for the second you say his."

James' fingers swirl elegantly atop my clit, and I reach for him to grip his shoulders instead of the mattress. "Oh my god, James—" I gasp, and he gives a soft, pleased hum against my ear. He pulls my hair again, harder than before, and I moan. "Oh my god, baby, oh my *god*—"

"*Come*, Davidson," Luke demands behind me, each syllable fragmented. "Come so I can—*fuck*—so I can blow already, because you've been *strangling* my cock, and I—"

James kisses the side of my neck, bites softly, and pulls my hair hard enough to hurt in the most delicious way. "Say his name when you come," he says again, his tongue licking the spot he'd just bitten. "And tell him to come inside you. You know he wants to hear you tell him to fill you up."

My body pulls rigidly tight and then tighter still, every muscle seizing until it burns. Behind my eyes, stars gather from the pressure of my eyelids. "Oh, *god*, James—" I say again, almost a whine, and then I feel it. The world shatters, and I shatter with it. *"Fuck—fuck, Luke—"*

Some incoherent nonsense follows, something that I don't even truly think about as affirmations pour free in relief. My entire body pulses with it, and blood pounds in my ears, although not so loudly that I don't hear the wet sound of Luke's cock thrusting more erratically than ever, or the raw, desperate sounds he makes as his own tension ratchets up further.

"Say it, Mills," James urges beside my ear as his hand releases my hair. The speed of his own breaths have increased once again. Truly, maybe they've never slowed. "Tell him to come inside you. Say it. He's waiting for—"

I'm helpless not to follow through. "Come, Luke," I plead, and Luke groans in response. "Come inside me. I want to feel you come. I want—"

He releases at that, and it feels that way even to me—like release, as he nearly hollers while pounding his way through what both sounds like something both desperately sought and finally acquired. Once, twice, three times, he slams into my body with the most force yet, each thrust deep and almost brutal as he pulses inside me, and then he sucks in a breath so intense that it sounds like it hurts. *"Fuck,"* he says, but differently than ever before. He sounds absolutely wrecked and yet wholly pleased, the single syllable broken and warm and rather shocked overall, and both the speed and strength of his thrusts wane as he chases the last vestiges of climax. Soon, his hands have softened against my skin, no longer clutching but instead stroking, and he bends to kiss one of the notches of my spine. "Holy *shit,* Davidson," he says, and he manages to make it sound like one of the highest compliments I've ever received. He presses his forehead to my back, groaning, and his tongue darts out to taste my skin. "I'm fucked. I'm *so* fucked. So very, very fucked."

James laughs softly against my ear, his fingers still stroking me through the end of my own orgasm. "Addicting, like I said," he mutters, and Luke exhales a laugh into my back.

"You weren't kidding."

I nudge James' hand away, and he withdraws it from under me. It allows me to stretch my bent legs flat, providing relief to aching muscles. "God, I'm exhausted."

Luke collapses with me as I fall flat against the bed, and with hardly more than a quiet grunt. "If that's my cue to pull out of you, I'm not ready. Not when you're still gripping my cock like you're determined to get more out of me." Yet he does pull out eventually, breathing a soft sigh that sounds like loss, and he presses a faint series of kisses across the bottom portion of my back that trail lower onto the curve of my ass. "I kind of lost my head a little," he says, his tone laced with a hint of regret, and each kiss feels like a follow up to that unspoken apology. "I didn't realize how tight my fingers were. You might bruise."

"I'm sure James has done worse," I tell him, both because it's true and to make him laugh. They both do, quiet laughter filtering out in tandem, and I roll over onto my back for a luxuriant stretch.

They both move after that, although I don't. James goes to fetch a towel from the adjoining bathroom, and he wipes up where Luke spills out of me without question or comment, just as he's cleaned thousands of his own messes. Luke watches the interaction for a moment, his expression rather strange, and then reaches for his shorts.

"Drinks?" he asks, and he barely waits for an answer from either one of us before he ducks out the door and latches it behind him.

James joins me on the bed, his body close but not quite touching mine, and he takes my hand in his. "He feels a bit weird, I think," he says quietly as he entwines our fingers together.

The beat of my heart has only just begun to return to normal, but it flickers a little faster at that. "Why?"

"Could be anything, really, but if I had to guess—" He kisses the back of my hand tenderly, the twist of his mouth thoughtful. "I'm sure there's an element of 'now what?' for him. I mean, I know there is for all of us, but...he's the odd one out here, or probably thinks of himself that way."

"With you two, I feel like the third-wheel more often than I don't."

James laughs, and his eyes crinkle in the corners. "Tell him that. That might help, actually." Again, he kisses my hand. "But...what do you want, Mills?"

I roll towards him, take in the cool scent of his neck, and sigh. "A nap, and then to go again."

"Right, and we'll do that, but—what do you want with Luke, and with me?"

The sudden seriousness of his voice knocks me off-guard. "What do you mean?"

"I mean—" He takes his hand from mine and brushes back my hair from where it sticks to the stubble of his jaw. A second pass of his hand feels more for his own pleasure, and then his fingers trail down my back in a time-honored caress. "You heard him. He's fucked, and it's because he's *into* you, and more than ever. I don't blame him. I was already crazy about you before the first time we had sex, but after that, I was *gone*. And—" He fumbles a little, clearly at a loss for the precise words. "The first time was great with you, but this—what we just did with him—it was...more than that. *Way* more. If this was my first time with you, and I thought I'd have to give that up—"

When he doesn't finish, I tip my head back to look at him. "Does he have to give it up?"

His answer comes immediately. "No. Not if you don't want him to. I'm fine with that."

"Fine with *what,* James?"

He looks like he chooses each word carefully. "Sharing you with him, your body and...your feelings too, because it would happen that way if we kept this up. You're already too good of friends to not fall in love with each other. It wouldn't surprise me if he's already halfway—"

"Love?" It flies from my mouth like a protest. "James, I'm not—I love *you.* You *know* that. I don't—"

"You can love two people, babe. It's not impossible, and... it's like I said. If it were anyone else, I'd hate it. But the three of us makes sense, at least to me. Knowing Luke like I do—" He shrugs. "I'd bet it would make sense to him too."

He offers me happiness on a silver platter, an impossibly brilliant future of laughter and lust and love that I've dreamt about for years, mine of the taking if only I'm brave enough to reach out and grab it.

"He wouldn't—" I pause, take a breath, and start again. "Why would he want to do that? He could get his own girlfriend. God, any girl would—"

James speaks softly, gently, as if revealing a deep secret. "He doesn't want any girl. He wants *you,* Mills." Bending, he captures my mouth for a kiss, one as gentle and soft as his tone. "All you can do is ask him, and all he can do is say no. If he does, we'll ride this out as long as he wants it—and I mean *ride* this out, because I have a lot of plans for you, and I'm sure he does too—and then we'll go back to just me and you. I'm good with that too."

So am I. I *am.* Except—

I'm also not, and I don't think he is either. Based on the careful way he watches me—like he expects me to protest, or perhaps wants me to—I can see that some portion of James' happiness hinges on my bravery too.

"I love you," he says, kissing me again. "So much. More than anything." He offers me another kiss, one that feels more final. "When Luke gets back, I'll go to the bathroom. Either ask him or don't. It's up to you, and I'll love you either way."

As promised, the second Luke joins us again, James takes the beer he offers, sets it on his nightstand, and disappears into the adjoining bath.

"You alright?" Luke asks, passing me a seltzer. He tosses himself onto the bed, bunches his pillow behind his head, and props himself up on one arm to take a swallow of his drink. "You're looking a little...off."

I *feel* off.

I roll onto my stomach, press the cool can to the side of my neck, and shiver at the sensation. "I'm fine," I tell him, and his eyebrow flickers, briefly raised, but he says nothing. "Just—"

"Is this the part where you start feeling guilty?"

"No," I say, and I hear him sigh into the neck of his bottle. It sounds unmistakably like relief. "What, did you think I would?"

He answers immediately. "Yes. You've felt that way before over a lot less. Sometimes you look guilty just because you catch me *looking* at you, and...I just did a lot more than look, and I'm still looking." His eyes burn against my flesh, trailing across my back, over the curve of my ass, and down my legs. "I'm afraid I'm not going to be able to *stop* looking now, or thinking, or wanting, or—"

"Are you actually? Afraid?"

His mouth stills, his lips held around whatever he'd meant to say next, and they remain there for a few breaths. "Of what?"

"Me. Us. This. Anything."

He glances towards the bathroom door. Why? To look for

James for help, or in fear of him reappearing? "Yeah. Yeah, I guess."

The rare glimmer of vulnerability, no matter how casually put, nudges at something in my chest. "Why?"

He sighs. "I don't know. Look, do we have to do this? I don't want—"

"James says you're going to fall in love with me."

His mouth doesn't just still. All of him freezes, including his bottle halfway to his lips, and it holds there as our eyes lock. Neither of us blink.

I add the next part quickly, to put the tension to bed for both of us. "He also said he's fine with it if you do, and that we can continue this, the three of us, for…for as long as you want, really."

The tension doesn't deplete. My heart continues to pound frantically in every vein in my body, and Luke continues to stare at me.

It doesn't take long for doubt to creep in.

"But if you don't want—" I begin, embarrassment flooding my system, and I start to roll over, to sit up, to simply get *away* from the situation and him, but he stops me.

"No, no—fuck, stop it, come here—" He sets his drink aside, pulls mine free as well, and then gathers me in his arms. He's held me before in the past, usually tucking me casually under an arm to joke with me, but never like *this*. Settling onto his side, he slides a strong arm across my back and pulls me flush into his body, and then he drops his hand to lift my leg to slide over his waist. "I—*of course* I want that. For fuck's sake, Davidson, I want anything you and James want to give me, but I didn't think—" His hand slides up my leg, up my hip, up my side, winds into my hair, and all with the ease of a gesture practiced many times, although he's never done it before. It doesn't matter. Things just *feel like* that with him—*everything* feels like that with him—and as it hasn't with anyone else besides—

Besides James. He simply feels like James—not that I don't know who he is, or that I overlook their differences, or that I think of them as one. But the way he makes me feel—the way we feel *together*—is almost identical, and it strikes me with the force of a sharp cuff to the back of the head.

James is right. I could fall in love with this man—in love with him *too*, right alongside my love for James. What's more, that knowledge hasn't diminished my love for James a bit. If anything, his endless, aching devotion to me—to me and Luke both—has only made me love him *more*. Yet I still have more love to give, and I want to give it to Luke.

"I could, you know," Luke says quietly. His thumb finds the pulse point along one side of my neck, and he strokes there, surely feeling my heartbeat thrum. "Love you, that is. Easily. I could love James too, even though that part isn't sexual. I mean, I already *do* love him. He's like my brother, after all, and you're—" He sighs. "You're *everything*, Davidson."

"*Oh*." It leaves my chest on exhalation, and Luke watches it go, his eyes flickering to my mouth. "So—do you want—"

"What do *you* want?"

I don't even have to think. "You," I tell him, and he sighs again with even more relief. "You and James both, together and separately, and—" I pause, hesitate on the brink of something deep and dark, and take the plunge. "Earlier, when you said you weren't going to want anyone else like you want me, I—god, Luke, I got *jealous*. It's selfish and awful and it doesn't make any sense, but—I don't want you with anyone else. I want you with *me*, with me and James, because I could love you too. I want—"

He growls, a sound yanked from deep in the pit of his gut, and he kisses me hard enough to bruise. "Fuck off," he says, licking his way into my mouth, and I can't hear the words as anything except a compliment. "Fuck *off*. You *know* I'm yours, or you should. How long have I wanted you? How long have I waited for you, for this, for something that might have never happened if James hadn't pushed us together? How much better is all of it—*all* of it, all of *you*—than I ever imagined? God, come here. Come here and *claim me*, Davidson. Show me I'm yours, because I *am*."

I shove his shoulder down flat with the bed and scramble atop him, nerves and exhaustion both things of the past. Suddenly, the future—both immediate and as far as I can see it—is so bright that I can taste it, and it tastes like Luke and James both.

"James!" Luke calls finally, after we've kissed until I've forgotten about all thoughts except those that revolve the beautiful man underneath me and the beautiful man who lurks just out of sight.

James exits the bathroom a second later, and I don't have to turn my head to feel him survey the situation. His eyes on our tangled bodies paint a distinctive path all their own. "So, it went well, I take it?" he asks, and I hear suppressed laughter, suppressed relief, suppressed *joy* behind the teasing words.

"Perfectly," Luke says as I kiss my way down the side of his neck. "*So* perfectly. I'll thank you later—thank you *both* later—but for now—" He groans as I nip at the base of his throat. "I promised her earlier today that she could do whatever she wanted to me after we fucked, which means—*god, Davidson*—that she's at your mercy like I'm at hers."

I hear James' sharp intake of breath, and turn my head in time to find his smile, already wide, grow impossibly wider. "Oh, good," he says, and with such heat that my body floods with it. His eyes have gone dark once again. "*Good.*"

CHAPTER 5

MILLIE

Come morning, I'm battered and bruised and more exhausted than I've ever been in my life. My body feels like it's been put through the wringer, because it *has*, and several times over.

I've also never been happier.

"There's no way—" I protest, half-bent over the kitchen island and fully clothed but also with my dress pulled up indecently high. Behind me, Luke seems intent on working me back out of my panties. "There's no way you can go again. You should be dead right now. You should *both* be dead right now. How many—"

"Watch me," he says darkly, and my core clenches at that. His fingers trace a feather-light trail across the center of my pussy. "Come on. Moan for me."

I do, despite myself, and my back arches uncontrollably.

Beside me, seated atop the counter with cereal in hand, James laughs. "You can't blame him, babe," he says, and he pets my hair in a familiar, loving stroke. "Not with how many times he's had to have thought about bending you over this counter. How many times, Luke?"

"I've lost count. Do you have any idea how—"

"Oh!"

The exclamation flies out from over by the stairs, followed by an almost-comical gasp. Quick as lightning, Luke pulls away from me, and I hear him swear quietly as I lift my head to find Annette and Cassie staring. They wear twin expressions of shock, their eyes pulled wide and their mouths held vacant, before Annette claps a hand over the lower portion of her face.

"'Morning," James says easily, twisting towards them. He takes another bite of Cheerios as mortification rises in my cheeks. "Did you sleep well?"

Cassie answers first. Sort of. "I—" she begins, but then she stops. "What?"

"Did you sleep well?" James repeats. "I did, when I got it. The three of us were up most of the night."

Slowly, Cassie repeats it back to him. "The...three of you?"

"Yeah, and on that—" James glances thoughtfully towards me, and then to where Luke lurks somewhere behind me. Whatever he sees makes his mouth jump with suppressed mirth. "I figured we'd keep our room, Mills, in case you want to spend the night with just Luke or with just me, but I know they're really crowded upstairs. What would you rather do? And, Luke, are you cool with us crashing in your room for the rest of the trip so the others have more space? I don't want to impose."

Oh, he's enjoying this. He's *properly* enjoying this, and—

As if on instinct, like the sight of James' amusement sparks something of his own, Luke snorts. "It's not an imposition if you snore less than you did last night."

"No promises, but—good. Great. We'll ask the guys and see if any of them want to move into me and Millie's room, although I doubt they will. We've spent enough time in there that—well, if they think about it, they're not going to want to get anywhere near that bed. Or that shower. Or that weird little ledge by the window. Or—"

"We get it," Cassie says. She stares at me, her blue eyes as sharp and penetrating as knives. "Is there coffee yet? Jesus, it's too early for this. I need coffee, and then—" Again, her eyes stab me with intense curiosity, a curiosity echoed behind her in the gentler angles of Annette's face. "We're going to have a *very* long talk, Millie."

We are, which means we'll have to get into the true thick of things, but at least we've passed the first hurdle.

Not only that, but Luke seems like he feels better for it. He smiles at me when I turn, although he waits for Annette and Cassie to collect their coffee before he kisses me. Although he'd kissed me hundreds of times the night before —quite literally—this one comes out differently still, both softer and more tentative than any yet.

"I'm happy," he says quietly, his fingers in my hair and his gaze as burning hot as ever, but bright with something else. It looks a little like awe. "God, Davidson, I'm *so* happy."

James repeats something similar mere minutes later, after he hops down from the counter to put his bowl into the dishwasher and promptly snags me in his arms. "It's going to be a good day," he says, his eyes alight with familiar, boyish excitement. "*Such* a good day. I can feel it already." Dropping a hand to my ass, he squeezes me gently. "Wear the thong bikini again, will you? I want to see Luke struggle with not knowing exactly how to treat you yet, and..." He winks. "It's going to be fun, watching the others try to figure out who left those bruises on your ass."

Oh, good lord.

I hadn't even *considered* that.

Want more **Beachside Ménage**? Cassie's story, *Competition*, is next.

Read on for an exclusive preview, or check out other books by Maisie Beasley.

COMPETITION

"To the victor go the spoils."
As college soccer stars, competition had come often and easily to best friends Kyle and Aaron, both on the field and in the bedroom. Across four years, any number of satisfied women had passed between their beds, caught up in a game between two dominant, demanding men set on being *The Best*, with no room for regrets.

Except Cassie.

Sassy, sweet, stunningly beautiful—and, most importantly, *their friend*—Cassie had unknowingly played a unique role in the long game of competition: the one who had gotten away, separately, from both Kyle and Aaron. For years, she has ruminated over her own regrets with the two

—and her own forbidden fantasies, as hot and torrid as the summer sun.

Now, years later in the midst of a seductive beach vacation, competition resurfaces, and more intensely than ever—not only for who will get there first, but who will get Cassie better…get her *off* better, that is. And, now that they've clued Cassie into the game, a new player emerges: Cassie herself, who seeks her own form of victory with her own prize in mind.

When it comes to competition, some win and some lose. But, in this case, can *everyone* win? The prize, at least, is clear: a new relationship, forged between the three, that promises a future of untold carnal pleasures—in triplicate.

∼

A PREVIEW OF COMPETITION

Chapter One
CASSIE

"So they just…share her?"

Listening to Kyle means plucking an earbud free. He sits sprawled across a beach chair inches away, his long legs trailing on powdery white sand and his head turned towards the nearby waves that lap at the shore. "What?"

He nods to his right. Several yards away, so close that her laughter sounds over the rush of the water, one of my best friends, Millie, kicks at the surf that surges around her hips. With great ease, our friend Luke picks her up around the waist and tosses her deeper into the glittering waves. He takes a moment to laugh, his head rocking back with it, before he dives after her.

Oh, and Millie's boyfriend, James, who doubles as Luke's best friend? He looks on with his own laughter when Millie emerges, splashes Luke soundly in the face, and then accepts the kiss Luke plants upon her lips.

Yeah. Only a few days have passed since *that* strange turn of events, and no one in our friend groups knows quite what to make of it.

"That's how it sounds," I tell Kyle, who watches the scene play out with blatant interest. Brilliant June sunshine catches in his hair, revealing fiery strands among thick chestnut waves. The same color carries in a close-cut beard that crosses his angular jaw, and also sprinkles across his arms, where many beach- and pool-side days have gathered a faint dusting of freckles. The most cluster around his muscular shoulders, which flex briefly as he leans his chair back to bear his face fully towards the hot sunshine. "Have they said much to you and the guys?"

"Nah." Kyle props a strong arm behind his head; the other lifts to shade his eyes as he turns to look at me. "They seem happy, though, don't they? Millie too."

"She should be. She's getting laid twice as much."

Kyle laughs; his broad chest jumps with it. "Jealous?"

Yes and no. Although unquestionably hot, I've never looked at either James or Luke that way. Yet, on the other hand—

Watching the three of them bask in delirious happiness has gotten old quickly, even if it's not had at anyone else's expense. It still *feels* at our expense, though, because, *God*, I need to get laid.

"I'm feeling a bit of that too," Kyle says into the pause that follows.

"What?"

"You know." He lowers his hand from his brow, and his palm across my hand emphasizes the tight hold of my towel between my fingers. "That."

My grip unwinds with a stroke from his fingers. Almost absently, he turns my hand over, spreads my fingers, and stretches his palm across mine.

"I could take care of it for you," he adds, an offer spoken casually.

That, certainly, is worth pausing my music for.

"Take care of *what* for me?" I ask, snatching my other earbud free.

He smiles a familiar smile, one that had turned many heads back in our college days—*too* many heads, really. The second our friend groups had merged, the sheer number of swooning girls that had followed him had gotten old rather quickly. "You know what I'm talking about."

"Probably, but I still want to hear you say it."

His chest jumps a second time when he laughs again. "I've got no problem saying it. You know—" He turns in his chair, angling his lithe body my way completely. His hand slips up my wrist in a soft stroke. "That party senior year, I always regretted—"

"We went to a lot of parties senior year."

"Yeah, but we only made out at one."

He's not wrong. Other times, we had certainly danced around it, and around each other, both literally and figuratively. We've always had *something* between us, although we'd only acted on it once. That night, he'd had just enough to drink to grab me in the hallway of his fraternity house. That night, I'd had just enough to drink to want him to do it, the potential destruction of our friendship be damned.

Yet it had turned out okay. In fact, we'd never spoken of it again.

"I still think about it sometimes," he says. Do his fingertips linger on the inside of my wrist, seeking my pulse? "Every time I see you, for sure, but also…sometimes it just hits me. The memory of it. I had no idea you could *kiss* like that, Cass, fuck."

My wrist comes free of his grip, first twisted and then pulled back to brush my hand through my hair. His eyes, as blue as the sky behind him, follow the motion intently. "That was a long time ago—*years* ago. Why—"

"This is the first time we've both been single since then."

It takes a moment, and a long one, to count back the years that have passed since we'd left our alma mater behind. Still, it hits me eventually. He's *right*.

"You really still think about it?" I ask, and his eyebrow twitches. One corner of his mouth goes with it.

"You don't? Or do you spend your time thinking about when you almost went home with Aaron?"

My hand flies over my mouth, and it stays there long after he starts to laugh. Heated words press into heated skin as I speak, and the accusation rushes out between quick breaths. "You *knew*—"

"Of course I knew. Aaron's my boy. We did everything together back then—soccer, classes, parties—and we always had the same taste in women. It wouldn't surprise me if he tried to take you home because he knew we'd kissed—what, the week before?"

Exactly nine days before, a number I still haven't forgotten. My conscience simply hasn't let me. College hookups had happened often and easily then, but something about kissing two best friends—and very nearly, *very nearly,* going further with both—had done something rotten to my insides. My own close friendship with each of them hadn't helped, and the possibility of all that could have gone wrong had kept me from dragging one of them off to bed—or both of them, honestly—even though they'd both offered. Extensively.

More dating and more hookups have happened since then, and, in between those times, I've regretted not taking one of them—or, again, both of them—up on their offers.

"Cass, are you *blushing?*" Kyle asks, his eyes dancing.

Hitting the solid mass of his shoulder once, and then twice for good measure, doesn't deter him. "I don't know if I've ever seen you—"

"It's not funny! I felt like *shit* over that, you asshole, and for *years*. Every time I've seen you since, I've felt—and, god, every time I've seen Aaron too—"

"You rang?"

Aaron's voice hits like a strike of lightning, and my phone tumbles out of my hand towards the sand. Immediately, Kyle begins to laugh, and my cheeks go, if possible, even hotter.

"Jumpy today, aren't you?" Aaron asks. Over the top of my head, he lobs a soccer ball to Kyle, who catches it between wide hands. Sweat drips across Aaron's forehead, runs down his neck, cascades towards his toned chest as he bends to rescue my phone, which he presses atop my thigh. His fingers remain there as he grabs his t-shirt off the top of my beach bag, and then he squeezes my leg faintly before he lifts his shirt to rub at the short, dark hair atop his head. "You're looking a little red, Cass."

Kyle tosses the ball above his head and catches it neatly. "Too much sun, I think."

Asshole.

"I'm fine." Shuffling through music helps occupy my hands, if not my thoughts, although I don't even take in what flies across my screen. "Go play with your balls, both of you."

A slow smile crosses Aaron's strong jaw. "Now, Cass—" he chides gently, and he bends one leg at the knee, his arms clasping behind his back to hold it in a long, practiced stretch. The thick muscles of his thigh bulge, drawing my attention like a moth to a flame. "You know I'd much rather you do that for—"

Kyle chucks the soccer ball back; it flashes in a streak of black and white over my head. "She knows."

I'm going to die. Officially. "Kyle, you—"

Aaron drops his leg to catch the ball. He manages, but at the last minute. "Knows what?"

Kyle ignores me. "Senior year."

"You're going to have to be more specific, man."

"She knows—"

Imagining how he'll finish that sentence convinces me to end it for him. "—that you've known all along that I made out with both of you. We really don't have to talk about it."

It's not that easy, of course.

"What, *that?*" Aaron asks. He drops the ball to the sand and lifts his other leg in a distracting, mouth-watering stretch. *"That's* why you're blushing? That was years ago, and —so what? Don't take this the wrong way, Cass, but—"

When he breaks off, his dark eyes look past me towards Kyle—for some sort of aid, perhaps?—but Kyle merely laughs. "No, go on," Kyle says. "I want to hear you finish that out. It'll be fun to watch you dig a hole for yourself here on the sand."

It's my turn to hit Aaron, a sharp smack that rebounds against the hard ridges of his stomach and probably hurts my hand more than it hurts him. Still, he nearly topples from where he balances on one foot, and that's good enough. "If you're going to start suggesting that I got around—"

Aaron recovers easily, with the grace of a natural athlete, and he clearly thinks better of continuing to stand. Instead, he settles onto the sand and stretches his legs broadly on either side of his body. His trunks ride up as he leans to the left, revealing a taut, tanned thigh that I definitely *don't* notice, and that I definitely *don't* remember wedged firmly between my own legs when he'd held me tight and kissed me breathless a few years back. "I mean, didn't we all get around? Except Annette. She was too well-behaved. Still is, if you ask me."

So well-behaved, in fact, that I'd bet my bank account that she's not actually sleeping nearby, and is only pretending for my benefit. Bless her.

"Not with *friends*," I insist. "Friends of mine, or friends to each other. That's how things get messy, and I—"

"Was that your only standard?" Kyle asks. "You know, I'd always wondered how Aaron tricked you into going there with him, because you're way out of his league, but if that was your only—"

Aaron laughs, low and deep; once again, the ball flies over my head. "Fuck off," he says, clearly unbothered.

I'm a bit more bothered. Just a bit. *"Both* of you can fuck off."

Kyle sits up to make the catch, and, although Aaron throws it high on purposes, he manages it neatly. "Do better," he taunts, before his attention returns to me. "Well, now that we have this out in the open—Cass, I need to know. Who was the better kisser? It really isn't—"

The answer slips from me quickly, and with more sarcasm than sincerity. "What, do you have no other way to know? Am I the only girl you've both—" It hits belatedly, and with nothing more than a quick glance at them both. "Oh my god, I'm *not* the only girl you've both gone for, am I?"

To their credit—or perhaps to their detriment—neither looks even slightly ashamed of that fact.

"What the *fuck*, you guys!" At the escalated pitch to my voice, Annette shifts a little. Not asleep, then. "Were you seriously out there trying to pull the same girls? What was it, some sort of—of *that?*"

I throw a hand towards the water, and both their heads turn with it, the motions almost in tandem. James has Millie now, her back drawn to his front and his hands pressed flat against her stomach. Yet he speaks over her head, addressing Luke more than her, his attention clearly split.

This time, Kyle laughs. "No. No, we didn't *share* anyone. It was more like—"

Aaron finishes the thought for him. "—a friendly competition, really."

Annette shifts again. I could almost swear that her petite frame shakes for a moment, as if she laughs.

With that, finally, I break too.

"Assholes." It bursts out savagely, but laughter follows, exhaled on a sudden, steady stream of relief. "You fucking—you *assholes*. If I'd known—do you know how much fun I could have had? How much fun I *would* have had? If you'd just told me you were trying to see who could land me first—good. *Great*, honestly. Or if you'd started it sooner, and not two weeks before graduation, you idiots—god, I could have stretched that out across an entire semester. Easily. I would have had you at each other's throats by the end of it, but you—I can't believe you *deprived* me of that, honestly—"

A grin cracks Aaron's face. "Cass," he chides again, as low and pleased as he'd always sounded back in school. It had always made me smile then too. "It wouldn't have been a true competition if you'd known about it."

"Really? Tell me—did the two of you play a lot of soccer without knowing you were at a match?"

For a moment, neither of them speaks.

"Jesus, you're dim. Both of you." Scooting to the end of my chair, I stand and stretch, and I take my sweet time at the latter. I know they'll both look, and, what's more, I *want* them to look. This time, now that we all know that we're playing, the game is mine. "You guys could have raffled off opportunities to take part in your little competitions. Do you know how many girls would have signed up? Your soccer groupies alone would have turned you a stiff profit."

Kyle spins the ball between his fingers, the same fingers

that had once tugged up the hem of my dress to cup around the curve of my ass. "You think?"

"Oh, I know. Anyway—it doesn't matter now. Thanks for the laugh, at least, since you both left me *seriously* unsatisfied back in the day. It was about time you guys gave me something. Annie, are you awake?"

Bless her again, because Annette pops her head up with impeccable timing, just as two near-identical sounds of protest erupt from my sides. "Did you say something?" she asks, pulling her cover-up from her face.

Bless her a third time, because she doesn't even try to sell it as halfway believable. Then again, none of us had probably expected her to. As Aaron had said, she really *is* too well-behaved.

"Let's go grab Millie and walk to the pier."

She rises unquestioningly. "Sounds good," she says, simple and sweet, and her smile looks it too. Without hesitation, she takes my hand and tugs me across the fine, warm sand, down towards the surf where Millie still frolics with her men, and away from the duo behind me who—

Who had nearly become mine, at least briefly, for a night or two or three. How had I landed in this timeline and not that one? Punishment for a past life's sins? Or retribution from a vengeful god? And yet, more importantly—

Is it a timeline I could potentially still realize?

"Cass—" Annette begins quietly, and her fingers squeeze mine. Although her eyes hide behind sunglasses, her voice imparts that they've widened, and significantly. "You know what they're going to do now, right?"

She sounds like titillation exemplified, and a swift, swooping sensation twists across my stomach. "Yes."

They're going to do *exactly* what I want them to do.

This vacation just got a whole lot more interesting.

A PREVIEW OF COMPETITION

PURCHASE COMPETITION HERE

~

ALSO IN THE BEACHSIDE MÉNAGE SERIES
CORRUPTED
(BEACHSIDE MÉNAGE BOOK 3)

"Lately, I can only think of both of you together, spreading me and sharing me and corrupting me and teaching me and showing me everything I've been missing."

Good girl Annette knows better than the lust after the unattainable.

Bryan, however, has long since comes to terms with his inability to get her off his mind.

And Grant? While he strives to help his friend get his match, he also can't deny that he often thinks about Annette too, and long into the night.

Opportunity strikes in the throes of a steamy beach vacation. Suddenly, Annette can't stop thinking about her two ripped, gorgeous friends. When pleasuring herself gives way to Bryan and Grant pleasuring her, the question remains: will Annette have the nerve to fulfill her wildest fantasy? And what will become of their friendship once the dust settles, their skin cools, and reality sets in?

It's time for nice girl to finish first.

Book three in the Beachside Ménage series, although each novella stands alone. Summer might be over, but your erotic fantasies don't have to be.

Author's Note: Featuring three points of view and chock-full of dirty dialogue, titillating foreplay, and steamy sex, *Corrupted* is a MFM romantic erotic novella that focuses entirely on the woman with no MM scenes.

ABOUT THE AUTHOR

Maisie Beasley writes romantic erotica that focuses upon mutual consent and shared pleasure—erotica written "through the female gaze," according to one reviewer. Whether that means two lovers—or three or more—may depend upon the story, but Maisie promises to deliver dirty dialogue and steamy scenes to keep you titillated until the final page.

Maisie loves hearing from her readers! You can reach her at maisiebeasley2021@gmail.com

Printed in Great Britain
by Amazon